**D0465228**

3

5

DATE DUE

| | | | |
|---|---|---|---|
| | | | |
| | | | |
| | | | |
| | | | |
| | | | |
| | | | |
| | | | |
| | | | |
| | | | |
| | | | |
| | | | |
| | | | |
| | | | |
| | | | |
| | | | |
| | | | |
| | | | |
| | | | |
| GAYLORD | | | PRINTED IN U.S.A |

**ROY**

**RASU**

**ron Aji**

**CITY LIGHTS**
**SAN FRANCISCO**

© 2002 by City Lights Books
All Rights Reserved

Translation © 2002 by Aron Aji

Death in Troy was originally published in Turkish as *Troya 'da Ölüm Vardi*
© 1991 by Metis Publications, Istanbul.

Cover design by Rex Ray
Book design by Elaine Katzenberger
Typography by Harvest Graphics


Library of Congress Cataloging-in-Publication Data

Karasu, Bilge.
    [Troya 'da ölüm vardi. English]
    Death in troy / by Bilge Karasu ; translated from the Turkish by Aron Aji.
        p.    sm.
    ISBN 0-87286-401-4
Aji, Aron, 1960– II. Title.
    PL248.K33 T713 2002
    894'.3533 — dc21                                        2002024170

**Visit our website: www.citylights.com**

CITY LIGHTS BOOKS are edited by Lawrence Ferlinghetti and Nancy J.
Peters and published at the City Lights Bookstore, 261 Columbus Avenue,
San Francisco, CA 94133

*To Gerar, and Joyce, always . . .*

*a.a.*

# CONTENTS

# BIRTH

Deep inside the creation, the pain of searing iron. The beast staggers in shuddering darkness. Even the heart renounces the unworthy moment. A warm sensation. Yellow, liquid, raw. Always rawness . . .

The litany of hours passing, one inside the other. Corpses. Countless. Rows and rows of corpses. Blood. Soil. Blood-stench soil. Death's visitation hours.

One scream—one—one. The iron pushes deep. Deep darkness, endlessly shuddering. Life fights to escape the iron. The bearer as blind as the borne. One more time. Against everything. The woman.

Then the dust. Under the sun. The heat. Iridescent. To walk the dusty road, as if endless (one, two, one, two, one—spasms, heat, charcoal heat, liquid heat, fire—two, one, two, one, two) to move through heat and more heat. In search of cold . . .

Caught in the scream, the beast staggers. Futile. Futility. Futile hours. A throbbing. A cloud, hushed, calm, free of pain, moves above the dusty road toward where there is less heat. Mother. The color of clouds. Joy. Oozing. The moist passage at the opening, the joy of quiet death, oozing.

The sun above. The creation still in the dark, yet to live. The sun scorches the shadows from above. Defeated shadows, shadows dissolving, turning to dust, shadows dying. The road. Hot. Still. Endless. The chafed calm of dust motes rising, falling.

An odor. Female. In the dusty, scorching heat, the odor of flesh oozing, bare, rancid. Regeneration still far off. The coolness of stones dissipates in the wind. A stirring. Contraction then release, tightening then widening. Release. Iron. The flesh splits open—the odor of flesh sh sh—parched, thirsty, drained of its excess water.

Underneath the stones, the wind stagnates. It gathers heat, dust. The stirring now becomes a push, the push of release, something akin to will. Slowly, slowly, beyond the heat, the drought, the dust . . . The sudden sweetness. The cool's soft . . . Soft. Nothing else. Cool. Soft. Equal. The first stirring still inside the belly. One emerging from nothing. Laughable. The cool air recedes, grows hazy again. Time begins its rounds of knocks against the tightening that time has ripened. Along with the heart. One, two, three, four, five . . . The count begins. Along with the unknown, hazy, fragrant light, past the verge of darkness . . .

The road is long. From trough to trough, one after the other, water gathers in pools of green, courses from trough to trough, spreads. The road shortens: abundant dissolution, joyous ripening. To flow through and through. To believe in the newness of life alongside death. To fall suddenly from the coolness of stones into the scorching belly of heat, then to retreat. To feel the round round reach of the stabbing push to fear it will stay buried inside the torn flesh to fall feeling its blood-soaked smell its throat-ripping swell to fall through the passage the tremors the oppressive heat the murmuring blood . . . The woman . . . The emptying. The easy, the very easy end of all emptying. The soft scream—long-awaited, unknowingly—that moves the stones. A boy, the first child. Toil. The woman reclines. Restful calm. The sea, washed in its own light.

Beguiled by birth, the male feels hunger. Insatiable hunger. The hunger of another birthing, of another impotence, exhausting, fatal.

1952

# ENTERING SARIKUM

I hadn't closed the curtains before going to bed. The sun hit my eyes as soon as it rose on the horizon. It was little after five-thirty. At first I considered taking a quick swim, but then decided against it. I would walk instead. The desk clerk was busy sleeping through the remainder of his shift. The teenage bellboy standing by the entrance was full of yawns himself. Six hours before, when he greeted me, he'd been disappointed that I had no luggage he could carry to my room. Avoiding eye contact, I left the hotel hurriedly. The pavement had started to dry, but I knew that the road ahead—if still unpaved, I thought to myself—would be muddy.

I tried to forget that I had walked in pouring rain all the way from the train station and stood in front of the clerk with my clothes dripping wet, looking like a guilty man. "Thank god I knew my way around; otherwise, I'd have been doomed," I had repeated while asking for a room. "You're lucky, sir," the clerk had said, "if it wasn't raining so hard, the hotel would be full!" It hadn't occurred to me at all that finding a room might be difficult. I hadn't thought that the brand-new, opulent Sarikum Hotel was the product of a greatly transformed Sarikum. Still, I wasn't willing to be overly grateful about my luck. Arriving on the last train and without reserving a room was a mark of my practical wisdom, I told myself, and went to bed.

I was in Sarikum once again. Just like years ago. But in a different room. A hotel room, strange and new. In fact, it was this strangeness, this newness that had made me apprehensive for so long. Hadn't I delayed my visit because I was afraid I wouldn't find a brand-new room for myself here? Yes, this hotel room was new and it would be mine for the next three to five days; yet at the same time, all the friends and acquaintances I would encounter in these three to five days would try to drag me back to the old days, to the old rooms. "Perhaps I can leave Yaliburnu and move here," I thought, surprising myself. I wasn't done with my life in Yaliburnu, my world there. In any case, I had to put these thoughts aside and see Sarikum.

My feet suddenly felt heavy. I was on a dirt road. Sarikum's clay soil was again sticking to the bottom of my shoes, making me look taller, giving me an awkward, painful gait. This was the road to the lighthouse; soon I would reach the outskirts of the village. Funny that I still thought of the place as a village. One would even think twice about calling it a town now. The lighthouse appeared in the distance. I realized this was the first time since leaving the hotel that I had raised my head to look at my surroundings. The sea had an orange glow. In the muffled dawn of orange and bluish gray, the shape of the lighthouse assumed a softness and looked embedded there—amid the vague colors—as if gently pressed in place by a thumb. Nearby, the yellow wheat bowed and bent, as always, rustling in the breeze. I walked the narrow road toward the meadow beyond the wheat fields. I wanted to see not the lighthouse, but our house. Still, I would meander and take the long way.

The meadow was golden yellow, dry, covered as always with barley and foxtails.

I would walk to the railroad tracks, then take my old path home from there. I would be greeted by the cool, sparkling white house that stood in front of the sun-baked meadow . . . I was day-dreaming.

I needed to stop at the Friends of Sarikum Society to see the chairman around eleven o'clock. I wanted to congratulate him on his idea to organize the Sarikum Festival to celebrate the establishment of the society. I had to thank him for remembering my father after all these years and for sending him a personal invitation, addressed to "My Esteemed Friend." I would explain that father had died eight years ago, that for the past five years I had been living away from my mother. Perhaps I would tell him that it was my mother who had given me the invitation. I would tell and explain all this, fine, but one thought troubled me the most: Mr. Çuhaci, this man who used to bounce me on his knees, would be interested in my life, he would try and sift through it as much as he could, wishing to know every little thing that had happened in the intervening years. "Never mind, just a couple of days, he won't have enough time to bother," I told myself, managing to let go of the thought for a minute. It would be better if Huseyin Çuhaci didn't know that the invitation was just an excuse, that after years of nostalgia, I had already decided to visit Sarikum one of these days.

A train whistle sounded in the distance. The sun was rising. I stepped on all sorts of wild plants whose names I didn't know. They gave off a gentle fragrance. I took the narrow gravel path leading to the train station. Walking, I tried to rub off the bulky clay that had hardened on the bottom of my shoes. As the sound of the train approached, I made it to the part of the path that was lined with houses and lawns. There was no use in trying to keep up with the train; I couldn't. The smoky roar calmed down near the station, briefly turned into a murmur, and gathering strength again, hurried on. It was already far away. I stood and watched the silent smoke clouds break up and dissolve in the air. The sound faded, then died somewhere in the distance. I resumed my walk.

To my right were vines: hook-fingered, twisting, stretching. They still bore the look of winter's leafless, fruitless poverty. Here and there, patches of morning fog hung in the gnarled lacework. I stopped. In my travels over the years, I have often leaned from train windows, trying to catch this morning scene.

The vines were barren. Vile, overtaken by death. They reminded me of the dwarf fortune-teller who had once lived in a hut somewhere around here. Rahime Hanim, too, was vile, she had done much wrong in her life. "She must have died by now," I thought.

I passed through the silence of houses. I was at the station, the place where the soil was coal dust and the stones were coal particles. It was completely quiet. I walked to the street.

The street, too, was quiet, full of sleep. Now and then, a window would open sleepily but remain dark, vacant, as if ready to plunge back into sleep. Yet, as I walked among them, many forgot their sleep. I saw women gazing out reluctantly between the curtains; then their bodies appeared, bending, leaning out. Walking past the windows, I saw the women pulling back; but afterward I sensed them reappearing—the looks, the curved, puzzled lips. None of these women could recognize me.

I couldn't recognize them either. They would have moved to Sarikum after we had moved away. As I left the street and walked to the meadow, I tried to forget the women. Sarikum always made its residents resemble itself, that's how it was.

Our house stood on the meadow's edge, glowing white. I crossed the field, trampling the plants. The dried yellow weeds, the small constellations of fleshy green leaves, the thorny, smooth, flat, clustered, twisted, strange plants, those that my old teacher had introduced to me as the plants of grassy lands. The purple, pink, blue flowers on sad, famished stems. All, I trampled on all of them with diligence and wild desire, burying them in the mud.

I wasn't looking at the house as I walked. I always approach my loved ones like this. At first I scan the surroundings, then fix my gaze on them. A shiver overtakes me. My beloved looks even more beautiful, more precious, more overwhelming than in reality. At times, I'm afraid of being overwhelmed. "So much beauty is sinful, unforgivable!" I say to myself. I try to go on living. I can't . . .

I stood at the end of the field. The little huts in front of our house had been transformed into concrete houses. My eyes still fixed on the ground, I took the stone path; not a single stone seemed changed. Just then, I raised my head as if in defiance and looked at the house. I tried to look without remembering. Fikret's home, Nebahat's home, both stood steadfastly in place. Their roof tiles were perhaps more worn out, the window shutters warped further, and the wood slats more weathered, whereas our house looked just the way we had left it: white, freshly painted, bright. Even the door was still red. The upstairs windows were draped, in sleep. I didn't know the new owners. "Perhaps tonight at the festival we'll meet," I thought. Then a sadness came over me: What would be the use of meeting?

No one was outside. Even though it was almost seven o'clock, no one on our street had started cleaning. I found that odd. Were they all strangers? Did they only come to spend the summers? I decided I could figure it out later. Turning the corner, I took the road to the gardens.

No gardens anymore. Houses, big and small, with or without lawns, had taken over. I walked. The doors, the windows seemed caught in imperturbable sleep, even though the sun flooded the rooms with light.

Only cats wandered around. Serious, pensive. I tried to call a few of them. The bravest among them stopped, as if weighing my

call, but ran away. The others had already disappeared. I was saddened. I thought I recognized some of them. Their race had apparently survived.

I turned left suddenly, as if prodded. In the opening between
two concrete houses, behind the two plum trees was Dilaver
Hanim's house. I stood still.

I wondered whether anyone else besides me knew what was
behind the house. Who else knew about Dilaver Hanim's patients
back in those days when she used to sit by her street window and
tell us stories filled with blood and violence? I remember one particular morning years ago, when I left for the gardens before anyone
else was awake. Later, it started raining. At first, I didn't worry.
When it turned into a downpour, I wanted to return home but it
didn't seem possible. Rushing through the plum orchard behind
Dilaver Hanim's house, I found shelter under the awning of her
back door. Cats circled around my feet. The house was quiet. The
rain started to come down even harder. But the downpour was the
least of my worries as I tried to find a place to escape the widening
puddles and the mud. If I were to return home now, I would be
scolded twice as hard. All of a sudden I noticed the cats disap-
pearing one after another as they turned the corner of the house. I
decided to follow and ran after them in the ankle-deep water. As
soon as I turned the corner, I found an open basement window,
hidden under the ivy. With difficulty, I squeezed my way inside.

I sensed the sharp smell first. When my eyes got used to the
dark, I saw the incredible sight. Amid the smell of bird droppings
and the sharp animal stench, stood a glass cabinet. It was identical
to the glass case that Reshit Efendi used to sell his pastries at the
station. A huge cabinet with wheels. It was so strange to see in
Dilaver Hanim's basement a replica of her husband's vending cart.
Then, inside the glass partitions, I noticed things stirring. I moved
closer. The cats swarmed around my feet. When I looked carefully,

I was seized with nausea. There was an animal in each partition. A kitten, a frog, a sparrow, a pigeon, a mouse, a snake . . .

Now I think the snake couldn't have been poisonous. A garden variety.

All the animals were wounded, crippled. Some had ears missing, others their tails, some were blind, others limping. One of the birds had a broken wing. And the snake was wounded in the belly.

An animal in every partition. I can't remember all of them now. But I remember noticing that none touched another.

I don't recall how long I stayed inside the basement that day. When I left through the window, it looked like the rain had stopped long ago. The sun was out and the insects were buzzing.

I never told this to Dilaver Hanim. Not even to her son, Mushfik, even though I used to peek secretly through the window, and once I saw Mushfik speaking to the animals, feeding them one by one.

I shook off the memories. Passersby were giving me strange looks. Cats had gathered at my feet; my feet had grown heavy, walking required effort. I was thinking of Mushfik. I had heard some time ago something to the effect that he had gone mad and had been hospitalized.

I thought I would find out what happened. I had to see Dilaver Hanim, kiss her hand—if she was still alive—would she even remember?

I reached the end of the street. More new homes were being built here. I walked around the lime pits, the broken cinderblocks, through cement dust. I heard a piercing meow. Then we met. A little ahead of me, it was wandering among the bags of cement. It was hard to tell its color, its coat was covered with sticky lime flakes, dirty, yellowish. As I approached, it raised its head. In its eye sockets, there was only thick puss. Blood-soaked, glistening, draining down its nose.

I held the kitten by its neck and carried it to the corner of the last plot of land clear of pits or scaffoldings. If it stayed in the plot, it had a chance to live. But I was sure it would come down to the street. It would tangle itself under someone's feet and be trampled. There was nothing I could do.

I turned and looked at the street again. I could distinguish the homes built during the war still standing among the new houses. The war, too, had passed through Sarikum.

It wasn't eight o'clock yet. I hoped the old fisherman's cafe would still be standing by the shore, but just as I was about to head off in that direction, I was startled.

Fikret was running toward me. Shouting, laughing, waving his arms . . .

1953

# THE FIRST OF THE SONGLESS NIGHTS

That morning it rained only in Sarikum, as I learned much later.

For us, the day turned out to be somewhat different from all others. It was cool, oppressive. For the first time in months, Sarikum could smell the rain, taste it.

At first, we sat on the front steps. They pulled us inside when the rain got heavier and our hair was soaked.

Grandmother was alone in the house. The way she dried my hair always felt like a punishment more severe than my mother's scolding. She was rough, yet I loved her so much; I wished that her hands would be the only ones to chastise me.

I was forbidden to go outside until the rain stopped, but Fikret, who was much older than I, could come over. Once he, too, was inside, Grandmother closed the door. We were now at the rain's mercy.

Fikret had been circumcised just a week ago; in the few days since, he had already begun to seem older to me, much older, like a grown man. Our age difference had never worried us before; I'd never thought of the six years between us when we talked until that day.

As Grandmother slowly climbed the stairs, Fikret pulled me

into my room. Closing the door, he knelt down and, reaching underneath the bed, pulled out the box of toys that contained the red locomotive, the green wagon cars, and the shiny steel rails. I always felt that he had more right to play with the train than I did. His father was the chief at the Sarikum train station.

I remember that I quickly relaxed, feeling Fikret's one week's worth of seniority evaporate. My spirits recovered and we lost ourselves in play.

When we tired of playing, we laid on the floor and read books. The sunlight pouring into the room slowly brought us back to Sarikum from distant islands of daydream. Now no one could hold us back. Except that we had to wait by the door for Grandmother to release us.

The meadow stretching in front of the house was saturated. We tried running until our feet were weighed down by mud and then we could hardly walk anymore. Like us, the other children also wanted to talk about the day's captivity, our first in a long while. When we met up, everyone sounded as if he had just discovered his house and tried to describe his room to the rest of us who weren't familiar with it.

We paused briefly, turning our gaze toward the meadow's edge, surprised by what we saw. I can still remember the puzzled looks on everyone's face.

The twins, Çetin the First and Metin the Bear, were riding their new bicycles through the mud toward us. Those bicycles hadn't even touched the yards in dry weather; they had seen no path other than the paved station road and the stone sidewalk. Çetin and Metin had been circumcised two weeks ago, and the bicycles were their wealthy father's gifts to them. For days, the overgrown twins had paraded around on their bikes, and although they pretended not to mind our name-calling, "asphalt boys," "show-offs," they threatened to beat us up one of these days.

The bicycles were nearly grounded in the mud. I was wondering if the time had come for our beating. The asphalt boys realized their helplessness and got off their bikes, deciding to drag the mud-caked wheels along as they came closer. We waited, as if for something urgent. I was a little afraid myself, and no one among us dared to tease them.

When they arrived, Çetin opened his arms as if to hug us all and said, "The Germans have invaded Poland." We remained silent. Metin handed his bicycle to Çetin in a brusque manner befitting his large body and came closer. His arms akimbo, he yelled, "We're telling you a war started, don't you get it?" adding proudly, "Father heard it on the radio."

At the time, only two homes in Sarikum had radios: theirs and the Çuhacis' famous twelve-room home crammed with their large family. So we understood the twins' pride. Even mom and dad went to their home not to visit but "to listen to the radio."

We were standing at the meadow's edge. Nobody spoke. Indignant at our silence, the twins pulled their bicycles to the side of the road, the gravel road full of big stones, and began cleaning the wheels with sticks.

A war had started. Just as I had seen in history books, in pictures full of horses, clashing spears, corpses scattered in a field.

We all began talking at once. I showed off all the geography I knew. Even before the twins left, all the countries and cities had been named. Everybody said something. I looked at Fikret. He was quiet. Then, without saying a word even to me, he began walking toward the station. He looked depressed walking, instead of running as he usually did. The twins seemed undisturbed, as if no one in their family felt saddened by the news. I couldn't understand; I ran home.

Grandmother was laying on the sofa in the living room. I remember running to her and telling her in one breath all I had heard from the twins and the others.

She got up abruptly. "So it's war? Again? The Germans again? Accursed race, they haven't had their fill already?"

She didn't look at me when saying these words. She didn't seem upset, but her eyes had filled with tears.

Afraid of making her angry, I went and sat in a corner of the stone porch. She could have gotten mad that I was sitting on bare stones, but I didn't think of that. There was a war, after all.

I knew my mother didn't like the Germans either. I would learn the reason much later. She held them responsible for my uncle's death in the First World War.

"We're telling you, the war has started," Metin had said.

Yet, the war couldn't have started. His father had heard it, and on the radio, too, but it had to be a lie. Didn't Ataturk, the father of our country, say, "Peace in the nation, peace on earth"? I had just read it somewhere. He did, but would the Germans listen to our Ata? Yes, he was dead, but didn't the German soldiers participate in the funeral procession last year, swinging their legs like scissors, wearing helmets that reminded me of my uncle's bald head? So it wasn't as if they didn't care.

Still, they obviously hadn't followed his decree. Perhaps Grandmother was upset because of that. She had every right to be. Then again, perhaps the radio had lied. Or perhaps Metin and Çetin had concocted the news. No, it couldn't be; they wouldn't have ruined their brand-new bicycles just to pull a prank like this. The news was true, absolutely.

So, what our Ata had said couldn't tie the hands of those Germans. Was it because he was dead?

I remember how I sat in the corner of the stone porch, little minding the cold slowly working into me, reliving the days of the funeral last year in a state that, now, I would liken to drunkenness.

I saw again the avenue that stretched from Taksim Monument to the War Academy and the slow, somber river of people. Our house was in front of the monument. All day long, the crowd never left the monument. There was a girl on the podium, crying, her face awash with tears. But her voice was calm. "We will never abandon your path," I remember her saying. "We will never abandon your path." The crowd responded with uproar and applause, I think. She had said a great deal more, but all I remembered was, "We will never abandon your path." That afternoon, my father walked me toward the War Academy. I looked at the faces in the crowd. Their mouths, eyelids looked heavy. Flags draped the entire avenue. I pressed my face against the flags as we passed underneath them. There were torches in front of the War Academy, and from time to time, a stern soldier with a metal jug would pour something into them. The air was filled with smoke. I felt heavy inside. The crowd was crying; I was unable to cry. I had given up trying. I couldn't force myself. Still, something was stinging my eyes, tightening my throat.

I understood the phrase, "We will never abandon your path." The Germans had abandoned our Ata's path. Obviously, neither the First World War nor the War of Independence had been enough to set things straight. I didn't understand more than that . . .

I remember that Grandmother's approaching footsteps startled me off the stones. We had to eat. I had forgotten the time.

Grandmother sent me out to buy bread. She tucked the money in my hand; I put it in my pocket quietly. Once outside, I no longer thought of Ata.

The midday sun was trying to dry out Sarikum. The streets were full of sweat, the soil was yielding, the stone walls were damp, a vaporous film hung suspended just above the roof tiles. Sarikum was enveloped in mist. I walked, neither hopping along the stones, looking over at my friends playing in the meadow, nor even wondering about the magazine Fikret was holding as he turned off the station road onto our street.

I thought of the Polish much later. Since I could imagine no war other than our War of Independence, I racked my brain wondering who would save them. I was walking without paying attention to the play-hungry cats. It felt hotter now. I was sweating along with the walls and the weeds growing beside them. Food odors came from open windows and doors. I heard the sizzling of eggplants, zucchinis, and voraciously inhaled the smells of fish and meats being grilled on porches. Cheese, onion, oil, melon, all smelled at once, mixing with a goat smell. Then it also smelled of grapes. Sarikum always smelled of grapes, so much so that it burned your throat. Since these smells rose on folds of heat up toward the blue sky every day, I presumed that people were feeling indifferent. But here and there I noticed a sense of heaviness about the faces, the hands, and realized I was mistaken. The meats were being turned on the grills, as every day, and moved to plates.

The loaf of bread under my arm, I passed by Dilaver Hanim's house with great interest. As always, she was looking out the window. I broke a bigger piece of bread than usual and put it in my mouth. Not missing a beat, Dilaver Hanim said the same words she did every day, her voice fresh and zestful, as if uttering the words for the first time: "Leave some bread for others, look at you! I'm coming to tell your grandmother."

She never left her house. Talking about leaving seemed enough satisfaction.

Dilaver Hanim looked the same. How could Sarikum have looked disturbed on account of the war when she looked the same: the woman who often called us over to her window and told us horrific, bloody, confusing war stories without noticing our mouths agape or caring whether we understood anything at all.

Back in the house, I told Grandmother my usual white lie: "The Matriarch sends her regards." "I send her mine," she replied. Yes, everything seemed as it did every day.

I remember that after the meal, pictures from books and magazines whizzed through my mind: the war dead, bloody shrouds, bandaged arms and foreheads, severed heads and arms piled beside rocks, tents, pipes, demolished walls. Grandmother was sitting by the window, tense, staring into the distance. Her silence meant she didn't want me to talk. She smoked one cigarette after another.

I didn't know why I felt depressed. Without Grandmother seeing me, I escaped through the gate and ran to the garden plots. I didn't want to see anybody. I wasn't afraid of the war, but it certainly was a bad thing. I felt sad. I didn't even call Fikret, whom I hadn't seen for hours. What he was doing then, I still don't know. I assume he was sitting at home and thinking deep thoughts. I will ask and find out one day; he can't have forgotten, I'm sure.

I walked among the plants. I would find what we called "snake eggs" near the roots, under the lower leaves, and crush them under my heel. Each time, I trembled with pleasure.

Suddenly, the sky turned dark. The air became saturated with the sound of insects. There, among the plants, it felt warm, sticky. Mom and Dad would be home soon. Running, I crossed the garden plots, the road, the meadow, then reached the pavement. From the distance came the sound of a train. I knelt down by a tree and waited. I must have dozed off. Dad and Mom were standing over me. I got up and immediately began to tell my father about the war. I remember telling him a jumbled story. The Germans, the Polish, the War of Independence, all got mixed up. Then I stopped. I wanted him to talk.

I waited, but he didn't talk. We crossed the meadow in silence. My mother began walking faster toward Grandmother who was standing outside the door, waving at us. My dad spoke then: "There is nothing to fear, son," he said, "not every war is a war of independence. The Germans are nasty. If the Polish can withstand them, it'll be good. If not, the situation could be bad, even for us. Don't be afraid. Men mustn't be afraid of war. It's tough. But it'll pass . . ."

He fell silent. I wanted to tell him that I wasn't afraid. Entering the house, he kissed Grandmother's hand. He didn't always do this.

They had brought me a book from Istanbul. I immersed myself in it. I didn't even want to eat. But my mother forced me to eat and then forced me to go to bed. I couldn't protest.

Something was bothering me but I couldn't figure out what. I remember it finally occurred to me in the twilight of early sleep: My father had not sung a song that night, for the first time . . .

1953

## THE FIFTH DAY

Then he came running to the fountain. I withdrew under the bridge. He brought his mouth and his palm to the spigot. His face was burning red. His forehead glistened. Sweat. Couldn't have been water. The dogs finally caught up with him and the sound of their own barking. They turned the corner, stirring up a confused dust cloud, and stopped in front of him. He was drinking water and didn't move. The two dogs sat on the muddy ground by the fountain, their eyes twitching. They waited for him, their tongues hanging out, trembling. One of them jabbed its teeth in its thigh; when its itching stopped, it went back to staring at him. He leaned back. Water spilled off his chin onto his chest

   his white chest

from his chest to his abdomen, tracing a transparent line down his shirt. He looked not at me but at the dogs. Then he quickly unbuttoned his pants. Don't piss, I couldn't say, shouldn't piss in the fountain, I couldn't say. His hand pushed inside his pants, came out full. He filled his other palm with water, held it under and whispered, "Drink, you're thirsty, too. We're both exhausted after so much running, my steed. Drink. Cool off." He didn't even look at me. I sat, tense. He watered it, tucked it back inside and buttoned up his pants. Then he turned his head and his eyes caught mine. The corner of his mouth curved up a bit, his eyes squinted. He bowed his head, smiling, then he glanced at the dogs, and they leaped up. He picked up a stone and threw it toward the meadow, and the two sprung forth like two stones after the stone, and he went running after them.

> the train
> in a ruinous roar
> passed over me
> I hadn't heard it coming
> even its whistle
> my temples throbbed under the wheels
> they fell silent my temples too
> fell silent

They were far away now. They didn't run toward the village, though he had thrown the stone in that direction. I was supposed to return to the village. No, I wasn't going to. I decided to run after them. I tossed the bunch of dill that Fikret's mother had asked me to gather for her. I stopped, wiped my sweaty palms on my pants. The dogs' voices were far away. Mushfik stood nearby. I walked slowly, then stood behind him. His legs glistened with beads of sweat. He turned toward me and said, "Let's go visit the doll maker." The dogs came running up, barking. We all sat on the grass. "Does your mother know you're here?" he asked. "Sure," I said. "Don't you go to school?" "The semester is almost over and we have just moved here; they'll send my grade report and I'll pass with honors." "Only three more days till vacation," he said, "that's why I cut school. Don't tell my mother. I'd make them bite you. Barut!" The gray one raised its head. Walking through the tall green grass, it came and rested its head on Mushfik's knee, fixed its eyes on me, blinked, then licked itself with its long, dry tongue. "I don't even know your mother," I said. "Maybe you'd try to tell once you do." He was staring at Barut. Both Barut and Sari had their heads tucked between his legs. Sari was barely visible in the tall grass. I looked at Mushfik and asked, "Who is the doll maker?" He got up; so did I; so did they in the tall grass, deep green. We walked to a spot where the grass was stubby, dry, trampled. We passed under another bridge. I had not seen this place yet, either from the village or from the other bridge that I had crossed twice so far. There was a tree. A plane tree perhaps. Under it, a low footpath. Suddenly, I saw the sea ahead of me. Pebbles, large, shiny, purple, yellow, a few green ones here and there, dusty, full of veins

> we walked on them
> we walked
> I looked

there was a large hut where the pebbles met the rocky cliff. In front of the hut, an arm, two legs lay among the pebbles. The arm and one of the legs were torn, dirty cotton with the corner of a rag spilling through the tear. The other leg was whole. Mushfik leaned over, picked up the whole leg, turned toward the sea and, stretching back his arm, flung it. The dogs jumped into the water. From inside the hut came a voice: "I hope you didn't toss the good one." "Yes, I did," said Mushfik. The voice: "That one made me angry, that's why I tossed it outside. It just wouldn't fit. But it still would have been useful. Never mind. Come inside. What did you bring?" I memorized every one of his words. "What was I supposed to do except throw the good one?" said Mushfik, pulling me by the arm, and we went inside. A man sat by the window, his back turned to us. "Who is this one?" he asked. "They just moved to Sarikum. They live near us. Fikret's neighbor." The man turned his head, looked, then resumed his work. Rows of shelves lined the walls. Stacks. Pots, pans, ropes, paper bags full of cotton and rags. In the corner of the ceiling near the door, bundles of arms and legs hung by ropes. I looked for the bodies. A bag full of dried grass, hay, and straw sat in the corner across from us. Over it, the bodies were piled, male or female, you couldn't tell, sad, armless like slaughtered chicks. Then

          did Rahime come by

          yes

          what did she say

behind the man,

          the same as always

          you're casting spells and selling

          them to kids with these dolls

          she says you destroyed

          the man from Istanbul

          you destroyed his family

          when his wife ran off with another man

          his daughter was holding

          one of your dolls in her arms

past the window, a shelf full of heads

          what did your mother say

          what would she say

          she laughed

          Rahime don't talk nonsense

          our son too once bought

          a doll from him

          has it hurt my marriage

          with Reshit Efendi

some had eyes, others didn't, glass eyes, painted eyes

          lady, she said, there must be an amulet

          under your shirt

          besides

          if he didn't cast a spell on you

be thankful
thank god that you look fine, she said
Fatma Hanim skinny as a needle
he drained her ounce by ounce
her too? Mother asked then
gave her money and sent her off
Fatma Hanim skinny as a needle
when she left our house
she probably stopped by his house
since they are newcomers

some had hair, others hats. The man suddenly turned to me. "Look here. You have to buy a doll if you have money; if you don't, you still buy one and bring your money the next time you come. You can't come in the shop and not buy." He expected me to reply, but I didn't. Mushfik was looking into my eyes. I stared at the doll maker. He was looking directly into my eyes. I remained silent. "You have to buy with your own money. I'd better not hear you asked your mother for the money. Because if she asks, you'd probably say you bought it from the doll maker Osman. If she asks where you got it, do you understand, if she asks

yelling
the heads with eyes
and those without
stare at him

where you got it, you say you found it in the meadow." He was roaring. "I am a man, not a girl," I said. "Men don't play with dolls." He glared at me. "All the kids in Sarikum buy dolls from Osman. They come and buy. Are they not men? Are you the only

of course I am a man
why else won't they let me cry at home

man? Hurry up and let me see your money." Mushfik again bowed his head, his eyes smiling, he gently moved his head as if asking me to buy. I searched my pocket and gave Osman what I could find, without knowing how much it was. He counted and took a couple of steps away from his table. "Pick one." The table was full of dolls in all colors. The one in front had its arms and legs in place but not its head. "No one can make these dolls like I do. I make the head, the arms, the legs separately, depending how I feel at the time, how I fancy them. Then I connect all the pieces with elastic bands. So they move. Though they tend to break quickly." I chose a navy blue one. Its dress was like a shroud,

> dad's mother had a white shroud
> white

I picked it up and looked at them both. Mushfik—sweet lips, eyes smiling—moved away from Osman, turned, "Let's go." We stepped out onto the pebbles again. The sea smelled cool, pleasant. "Mushfik, when you see that conjurer, tell her I'll come by one of these nights and rip her legs open," his voice was heavy. We moved away. "Okay," said Mushfik. By the sea

> if Rahime is the lead reader*
> I'm the doll maker
> I'd better not hear her
> calling me a conjurer

the carcass of a fish

> if I were a conjurer
> I would've stolen her clients
> evil dwarf

rotten, its black belly cracked open. The footpath we had just walked was behind us. The dogs leaped to their feet, their fur wet, muddy. They growled. Mushfik held my arm, squeezed it. "Let's skip stones." He picked up small pebbles, filled his palm; I put the

---

*A form of fortune telling. The reader pours hot lead in a bowl of cold water and interprets the shapes.

doll on the ground to pick up some stones. Sari attacked, snatched up the doll. So did Barut. Mushfik was skipping stones without looking at me. The dogs made no noise. The doll was torn to pieces. I couldn't call Mushfik. They spat the pieces around and lay on the ground again. I was repulsed. First I grabbed an arm, tossed it into the sea. Barut growled but didn't move. Then the other arm then the head then

> the head didn't sink at first
> the thin arms floated
> side by side

the body, I minced it into bits and scattered them in the water. Then the legs, one by one. Mushfik wasn't looking at the doll; he was still skipping stones. "Good for you," he said after each stone, "good. I'll be your friend." He threw his last stone. "Let's go," he said again. We walked by the water. The dogs ran ahead of us. We walked for a long time. Then, "Osman is a little crazy," Mushfik said. "Mom says so. When she first moved to Sarikum, she found Osman working for my father; he used to knead the pastry dough. Then one morning, it seems, he went to my father. 'I'm sick of it,' he said, 'I won't go to the buyer. Let him come to me. I don't know what, but I'll find something to do,' he said." Then they didn't see him for some time. Afterward, he began making dolls. "At first, he tried to sell them in the market. The dwarf Rahime claimed the dolls were charmed, so he was chased away. I felt sorry for him. Father was very angry, crazy, he called him, cursed." Then Mushfik saw him in the meadow one day, followed him and discovered where he lived. "I get all the kids to buy a doll," he said. "I got you to buy, too. I destroy their dolls whenever I get ahold of them. So they buy new ones." We stopped talking. Walked. The shore ended at one point. "Take off your shoes," he said. I did. I took off my socks, too. He had no socks. We went in the water. I gazed at

       crawling crawling
the tall rocks. "Don't dive," he said. "Just one more step and it gets
very deep. Three kids drowned here!" The pebbles

       pebbles underwater

       slippery

were difficult to walk on. Here, they were green, a little farther on,
dark with webs of seaweed. We walked around the jetty, then went
back onto the shore. He put his shoes on. I put on my socks. He
waited. I put my shoes on. The dogs went running off. Far ahead
of us were some swimmers. And farther away stood the lighthouse,
glowing white. We walked. Then, "Do you visit Osman often?" I
asked. "I do," he said. They liked each other a lot, he said. Then,
"You can go home from here," he said. He didn't call the dogs.
Beyond the pebbled shore, the ground rose in wrinkles of parched
red soil. He climbed up the cliff and ran. I could no longer see
him. He must have gone to the meadow. Suddenly, I felt my head
burning hot. I ran. Stumbled. Ran. When I reached the others, I
removed my clothes. But what if I got my underpants wet? If
Grandmother figured out that I went in the water—with or
without clothes—she'd scold me just the same. But she wouldn't
tell Mother. I would dry my underpants. The sun scorching, the
pebbles scorching. The noon hour. I don't know how to swim. I'll
learn. Both Mushfik and Fikret know how to swim. Now I'm all
dry. I should go home. Fikret's mom asked me to bring her some
dill. I wish I hadn't mentioned I was going to the meadow. Ah well,
what's to be done . . .

1954

# ONE OF THE ROOMS

The lighthouse illuminates the road again. Suat is already far away; he's swinging his one little fish. He'll reach the station in seven minutes, be home in ten. I turn around and stand on the beach road, waiting for the ray of light to fall on the boat. As the boat appears in the fleeting light, I toss my fish in the water. It falls with a thud, dry, hollow, hardened by death. It'll take me a long while to reach home, at least fifteen minutes. I feel lazy. I'm tired of walking. Father must be angry by now; he must have asked Mother to lock the door. Perhaps I should go to the hotel. I've never entered through its squeaky door that seems perpetually on the verge of yawning. For years, I've walked by it. When would I have had a reason to go in? I love my bed, my house. Perhaps I should say, my room. I only love my room. They've even made my room feel less enjoyable, it seems. The hotel will be strange, my clothes are quite inappropriate, but I don't care. Perhaps I can sneak into the house through the basement window if the door is locked. It's possible. No, the hotel, I should try the hotel. See a new room while I can. I have money, but no identification. Probably necessary. I can't exactly tell the clerk that I live in Sarikum, he'd tell me to just go home, he probably wouldn't believe the story about the locked door. Even if he believed me, he'd get suspicious. How would I ever walk by the hotel afterward? Best to tell the truth. I don't have my identification with me; I went out fishing, I'd say. Suat and I each caught a fish, just so we could say we did. He took his with him, so as not to return empty-handed. He'll bring it home, place it on the middle shelf of the cooler. If the whole family were to share it, no one would get more than a morsel. Or perhaps, he'll feed it to the cat. What matters is: Suat has gone fishing and has come back with a fish. My mother knows why I went out but, proud Dilaver Hanim that she is, she can't bring herself to say anything. In any case, I already tossed my fish. What use do I have for the dead meat? The people in the hotel would laugh if they saw me carrying one single fish. Not that it's anybody's business. I'll check in and go to bed. If they need personal information, I'll give it from memory. Besides, if I didn't live in Sarikum how would I know that there was a hotel in the old district? I'll just go. I must have been walking fast. My shirt sticks to my back. I feel the sweat running down my back to my waist. I arrive. Perhaps the man won't recognize me, since we don't live in the old district. No matter, I'll go in. All of a sudden, there are shooting stars. It's dark in front of the door; I breathe in the breeze and the smell of shooting stars, I feel them. Even in this heat, the door is kept closed. Inside, there is no sky; it smells bad. Is this how all hotels smell? Yet, I shouldn't let them know. I should act as if I'm used to hotels. Except for the clerk sitting under a pale sickly light, there is no one else around. I stand in front of him. He hasn't raised his head yet; he is reading a book. The door had squeaked when I entered. I lean over the counter. He is reading *The Art of Love*. I know the book; on the cover it says something like, "27 full-page illustrations." He should ask *me* about love . . . The shadow of his head begins to extend toward me. He is looking at my pants. They are stained, muddy—although he can't see the mud—wet, perhaps. I look at him. He stares at my hands on the counter. Perhaps he notices the smell of dead fish. My hands bear the dampness of salty water, the roughness of the boat's dusty surface, their calloused skin inflamed by the oars. But he cannot notice that. He continues to stare, trying to know me by my hands. Silly. He fixes his gaze on my belt. My shirt collar is open too far. Besides, I'm sweaty. Someone with a sweaty chest, where does he come from at this hour? He checks his watch. Almost one-thirty. He stares at my face, my eyes. As green as his. A moist green, as if he has cried or stared at the burning sand, at the burning sea. What do you want? ask the eyes. What would I? Annoyed, I look at the green. *I want a room.* The green grows deeper, rises toward my salty, curly hair, my sweaty forehead. I look deep inside the green. Single bed? he asks. Obviously he knows I need a single bed. What would I do with two? What floor? he says. Does he have to ask all these questions? Is it customary? I wouldn't know. The questions have nothing to do with the green of his eyes. Second floor then, he says. The hotel has only two floors. One night only, he asks. One, five, ten, man, finish your questions so you can return to your book, I want to say. The green again scans my whole body. Identification please, he says. *I don't have it.* My voice comes across too strong. Suddenly, he raises his eyes and his chin, as if ready to say, we can't book without it. Ask and I'll tell you, I say, I'm not a stranger. He almost says something, but decides not to. Lowers his head, your name, he says. *Mushfik.* I don't like being interrogated by a strange man, I almost want to change my mind and leave. I look up: The greens are once again fixed on my eyes, as if waiting. Your last name, he asks this time. I swallow anxiously. I should say Börekçi. *Mushfik Börekçi,* I say. He doesn't even pause while writing. He is not puzzled. He wouldn't be, even if I said Suat Çuhaci or Fikret Ünlü. Your father's name. *Reshit,* I say. I don't care. Then he asks, Where are you from? *From Sarikum,* I say without hesitating. I wish he would leave me alone. I speak, he writes; I speak, he writes. He stretches his arm, takes one of the keys from the hook, hands it to me. The torture is over, apparently. Second floor, across the stairway, he says. The room smells of sheets, toothpaste, sleep. I open the window. The sea, the star-studded sea fills the room. There is a cat on the adjacent balcony. I call to it from my own sea. It lifts its head, gets up, stretches, sits, lays down. I think I see its eyes closing.

I go inside, the sea recedes. I undress. I hang my shirt on the back of a chair. The pants can stay in the corner. The room is narrow, the bed wide. I sit on the cool sheet. Another traveler must have laid on it, left his warmth, his smell. But beds quickly turn cold. Hotels receive people daily, armies of people coming and going. This bed is no different. I'm in a brand-new room. For the first time, I am about to sleep somewhere other than my own room. To me, the place is new, yes, but to the clerk downstairs, was I new, any different? I was drowned among the names in the registry. Name after name, others yet to be written after mine. The clerk's green eyes. Eyes that won't sail away at night. I should have brought the fish with me, perhaps he would have quivered with longing. He probably sleeps during the day. But he wouldn't sail away, even if he goes in for a swim. He wouldn't be able to pull the boat away from the light. Yet, he would want to. Perhaps. Not perhaps: He would want to. His eyes looked sealed shut. Wouldn't even be able to notice the water rushing all the way to this window. This is the first time I'll sleep in a room overlooking the sea. There is an unfamiliar rawness about the recurrent beating of the waves against the shore. Strange. As if their work is finished, they beat idly against the rocks, rush, retreat, then beat again. The sound is like that of boathouses, the sound of the sea trapped under a roof. I am also under a roof. So is the clerk. His eyes, his liquid green eyes that glow in his pale, withdrawn face under the frail light. Once again, I experience the dispersal. A piece of me remains in his eyes. From now on, this piece, too, will be part of the gathering. He will be among those who have known me. But he won't be. He will forget. He will be among those I have known. I wish I had not come, never come. I would have moved on without recognition. Now he, too, belongs. Each time I gather the pieces of my being, I must find, I must remember the one left behind in his eyes, in the very depths of the green. I already paid for the room. I'll sneak out early tomorrow. If I can, I'll avoid him. I should escape early. I'll sleep among the stars, in the sea that flows in through the window. The clerk must be reading *The Art of Love*. I haven't even turned on the light; the sky's glow is enough. So there is also a closet in the room. To lie down in a new room, a thrill of sorts. The sheets, still cool. I'll sleep.

1954

## ROOM AFTER ROOM, THE WORLD

I knew they had been living in the Taksim district for the last three months, but had he not sent me the letter I wouldn't have thought to meet him in the garden of the church in Taksim.

Ten minutes before midnight, I shook his hand under the only electric light in the garden.

"Our resolve was pointless. We would've met somehow . . . And we will again . . ."

*The clarity of his letter. His words beginning just where he had left on our last night together, four months ago. He looks at me, his eyes in the shadow of his eyebrows.*

I didn't speak.

"This is the second time since my father's death."

He paused.

*As if the wind is making his voice tremble. On the evening after his father's burial, he climbed to my room, as though he had been waiting right under the window. Staring at the dark Bosphorus that flowed with summer calm, he said, "When I was watching my father's coffin come out, I decided to leave the church, I'm never going back." But his mother wanted him to take her to evening masses. Two days before they moved out of their house, on Christmas Eve, we took her to the small chapel in Yaliburnu and waited outside for her.*

"This is the second time. I wanted to be together tonight, too."

*As if feeling cold. His voice breaking.*

"Will we see each other again?"

*He still hasn't looked at my face.*

I made a vague sound.

Although he was obviously cold, he seemed cheerful. "Mother still resents you. Doesn't even want to hear your name mentioned. We sent Niko to boarding school and left the house in Yaliburnu. We now live behind Siraselviler, in one of Mother's aunts' houses. I've been working for a leather manufacturer for three months now. I quit school . . ."

*He pauses again. His voice barely audible. As if waiting for me to say something.*

"Mother likes it that nobody knows us here. In Yaliburnu, they still gossip about me, about us, it seems."

*The corner of my mouth twitches. In vain, I look for something different about him. His face, his voice, his heart, still the same. He must not have abandoned his books, even for a moment. He's absentminded now, the way he used to be, in his dark swarthiness.*

He was looking at the church's main entrance. At the long candle flames gently swaying above the heads of the crowd inside, some standing in the doorway.

"Like all of us, he was born of blood. Like some, he died in blood. Every year, during the four months between his birth and death, the hills in Yaliburnu are bluish white. At first it's snow, later come the daisies. You wouldn't even notice that the snows have melted and the ground is covered with the new blossoms. It's white everywhere, white it stays. Then there are the clouds, clouds that you lie under, pure white clouds that push the blue sky further away. Jesus' blood never colored those clouds. His blood is not human; it's divine blood; it flows and flows, but the hills stay white . . . always . . ."

*His mother shouldn't hear him talk like this. Even back then, she used to complain endlessly that he couldn't speak Greek well. The more he read, the more he would forget it, perhaps try to forget it. Greek must've become even stranger to him since he left school. He now speaks only the language of his books, as if reading.*

"Jesus' blood, it's beautiful but why should I care? Bloody Jesus, son of Miriam whose own blood flows down the five fountains, he's too remote. My blood is mine as much as my life. I wouldn't want them to drink of my blood . . ."

He stopped talking.

*He doesn't know what he's saying. His jaws are clenched to keep his teeth from chattering. Aleko, Aleksandros Vratsis, that is, a child raised in the shadow of those gathered around Jesus' blood, talking like this. Without fearing solitude, aloneness.*

On this night of Jesus' rebirth, his resurrection to eternity, the snowy cold of the April air made both of us shiver. *Yet in that hot land, Jesus had risen to heaven naked.*

"His Father will cleanse his blood. Watch how they'll shout for joy. Jesus will forget the mortal weight of his feet once again. His heart filled with love, but remote from us . . ."

*He sounds as if sleep-talking. He's cold, obviously. He looks at me. He's as beautiful as ever. But the corners of his mouth seem altogether downcast, earthbound. He hasn't yet understood that denial doesn't have to mean fear of faith. He wants to shout, I can see. His is the despair of youth.*

He looked at his watch. "Thirty-seven minutes since she went in, and she isn't about to come out."

Our cigarettes glowed in the darkness that remained indifferent to the river of candles inside. We walked a little. We stopped under the light again.

"I've been reciting your address in my head for four months. I couldn't make myself write. Then, since I had to bring my mother here, I couldn't resist. So I wrote . . ."

*This is not what he really wants to say; he's hesitating.*

"I wouldn't have gone inside anyway. I was justified . . ." He paused again. He didn't look at me. "Do you know what?" *His voice warmer.* "At first, I was afraid you wouldn't come. I was here at exactly eleven-thirty. Even though we were supposed to meet at quarter to twelve. My mother was puzzled by my impatience. But she couldn't imagine I'd be meeting you . . ."

*The air smells of candles. The wind carries the smell of flames on wave after wave. If I want, I can hear from here the sizzle of wicks, the murmur of prayers.*

"She is cleansing inside . . . praying . . . her head dizzy with the divine air . . . if she knew you were here . . ."

*He's agitated. As if he wants to stop talking but can't. His lips tremble when he begins to speak. His eyes, wide open, resemble those of frightened animals. He moves them from side to side, as if not quite sure where to look. The fear of showing his weakness.*

"It's been nine months since my father died. For nine months I've been distancing myself from them. I'm far away."

*He gathers himself. He's speaking with the certainty of youth. And soon the hard solitude of a man's world will swallow him whole.*

"But distancing is not enough. I can't express my separateness, my difference from them, by simply knowing that I have distanced myself."

*You can do it that way, I want to tell him, as long as you shape your life from that knowledge. But he wouldn't want to hear those words, much less understand them. He would grow suspicious of me, too. I, who taught him to avoid everything that he couldn't call his own. And wouldn't I be again telling him that only what he creates on his own can be his? I've remained silent so far. I should remain silent still.*

We smelled the wind again. Our heads sank deeper inside our collars. As we lit another cigarette, his lips trembled.

"You were there in the past . . . those four months . . . day and night, in those four months when I couldn't take myself away from you . . . Then, that Christmas Eve when you said you'd never see me again and left the house, I wouldn't believe it. Later, I thought you were running from the gossips. I assumed you left me because you were afraid of those who can't stop talking when they don't understand something . . ."

He gazed into my eyes. *He is smiling, I should smile back.*

"Yes, it was easy to believe that. I understand tonight. I'm free of you as well."

Could it be? Was he free?

He smiled again. "The new neighbors, they think I'm . . ." his index finger draws circles on his temple. "Let them. So what? Madness, after all . . ."

The crowd's murmur wafted over us.

"An hour ten minutes. It's been an hour and ten minutes since she went in."

"Don't be impatient, Aleko. You know it'll last a while, I don't need to tell you that. In Yaliburnu, even I had it figured out how long the mass lasts."

*Was this all I could come up with, as my first statement? I'm afraid it's too late, I've said it.*

I tried to smile, as if I had just remembered that I knew this. "Don't be impatient. Maybe you should've gone inside—"

"Yes. I should've gone inside. But I'm outside. And outside is cold . . ."

We walked again. *The back door of the church is cold, empty, dark; it remains a stranger to the lights and the joy inside, at the front door.* Under the light, he spoke again. "I'm cold. Staring at candles doesn't keep a person warm. I'm outside. What it's like to be outside, I don't . . ."

*Have to tell me. I know. But talk, don't stop.* I merely nodded.

"Inside, he's inside. The candles, the incense are for him. He's warmed up. With the breath of hundreds of people, with their warmth, their candles . . . If I didn't feel the pain, the longing . . . but I can't help . . ."

I was the one who told him, never get caught in the net of other people's thoughts, find your own path. And now, isn't he a slave to a life without reassurances?

"The flames, the way they keep the flames from going out, the waiting . . . I never saw myself as one of them. In my flight from them, I could have fallen into someone else's net. You protected me. At least I fell into my own net. You thought so, too, didn't you? I'm cold."

*He's losing it. We continue walking. Darkness dissolves, now growing lighter with our steps, now deeper, harder. His teeth are chattering.*

"If they hadn't made me feel that I was a bastard . . . if they had just let me be. If I hadn't realized my strangeness . . ."

*The light's glow on us again. He looks at my face. But absent-mindedly.*

"No point even in changing faiths . . . So be it . . ."

One of the side doors opens. *Candles in hand, they come out in twos and threes, their hands covering the flames. As it was in Yaliburnu. But there they all knew us, pointing at us and giggling. All two hundred insiders pure, and the two of us sinners. Perhaps they're angry at Aleko, but there must be some who think that at least he knows his place and stayed outside with the stranger instead of desecrating the church. He looks at the people coming out, his withdrawn face awash in light. But what lies ahead of him is room after room. He will get to know strange rooms. Move from one to another, feeling at home in none. He shivers, stiffens. Perhaps he sees the child up ahead. The child raises his extinguished candle to rekindle it from his father's. His father must have received his fire from somebody, and that somebody from the altar. Simple, right.*

He turned.

"One hour and forty minutes . . ."

Those who were standing at the entrance moved inside. Those with their flames longing for calm.

"Your mother will be out soon . . ."

*I wish I didn't say all these empty words. By tomorrow, he'll realize that I barely spoke. I hope he doesn't misunderstand. He speaks again.*

"I'm amazed it didn't snow."

*He avoids it.*

We each lit another cigarette. I didn't want to see his mother. He had his hands folded over his cigarette, trying to warm them. I told him to come and look for me in a few days. His eyes widened. Then I turned around and quickly walked away.

*It's cold outside. My room must have gotten cold by now.*

1952–1953

## AN UNRELENTING

solitude dwelt in men. After the cigarette, I said, "Women are not lonely. Women never are. Even when drinking." The smoke disintegrated. Solitude dwelt in men. The woman slowly emerged through the clouds of smoke, gliding. Then the lights dimmed.

We're going to separate anyhow; no point in meeting
The woman fixed her eyes on the birds tearing the smoke with their liquid flight. The birds circled in the middle. Then her arms moved through the darkness and joined the wings that obeyed the arms. The birds were not alone. They lived in her arms. Men were alone. The woman was among them, could not have been alone.

he is not the one leaving tomorrow I am
The Spanish dancers circled in the middle.

wildly thrashing as if yearning to escape without even imagining the futility of escape
The men, more birdlike than birds, awaited the moment when their feet would leave the ground.

while the women dispersed their bodies across the floor in endless gyrations

The sound of their heels was deafening. The men lowered their heads again.

> separation hung over us while the Spanish kept circling how come we can do nothing better than watch drink fix our gaze on the white-on-white embroidery of the tablecloth

The Spanish, tensed like springs, stomped the floor with all their might.

> gave up flying just for tonight

The men had briefly forgotten the woman. All of a sudden they remembered. She was drinking slowly.

> for her the evening is no different from any other, she drinks

and she watches as much as she wants. Barlini moved to center stage. We watched. Eight sticks at his ten fingertips, he kept the sticks balanced, spinning the plates at will. Plates, sticks, rolls, baskets, hats, all flew in the air, turned, spun, landed on his hand, on his forehead, on his nose, on his butt. Everyone watched him. He had his eyes fixed on his plates. He watched them, in an enveloping wave of solitude, even when the light danced around him. "His mother must have spanked him as a child," I said. "He probably cut school, trying to learn these tricks. His mother must've blamed herself, thinking her son became a vagrant." The smoke hung over my words. Then I fell silent.

> all three of us were drinking probably to avoid laughing at these idle words

He smiled at me with a lonely corner of his mouth. Best not to talk.

> it's not proper to stall solitude but one must think of tomorrow the place a hundred steps ahead of us where we will go our separate ways not even tomorrow today in eighteen hours sleep would both break and prolong these eighteen hours

We were amazed.

> I will never be able to see anything better than these three
> mulattos I know bebop I know this kind of rhythm the body
> can't do more than this they are flying the small woman the
> wiry men all of them are flying without landing

The woman was immersed in a gratifying sorrow. The men were
back to playing the blues on their instruments. Some danced in the
middle.

> we are alone and all of a sudden this cat just jumps on my lap
> it's shedding its yellow fur spring is here the cat will drown in
> its own purring even in this strange place the cat on my lap
> is not alone

The once-distant whistle of the train now sounded closer. Right
outside the walls, the chimes announcing the arrival. Money
changed hands — given, received. The wagon car was dark inside.

> outside the rolled-down windows I see death along with
> spring in these months of dying this year also we will die he
> is too drunk to think of tomorrow true maybe I also drank
> too much first at home then at the bar but I am thinking of
> tomorrow

We needed to know that we would die. I have made a habit of
crumbling through one death after another. A habit of feeling more
impoverished after each death, of preparing each death at the very
moment of its birth, of being swept away and knowingly, of awaiting
death even in the briefest moment of satisfaction. Death, the companion. I bought the ticket a few hours ago. But since yesterday I
had been saying that I bought it. I need death. Let the two of them
marry. I seek death. The time before separation always gets dis-
rupted. One stares blankly at the tearful eyes. Smiles are exchanged,
then handshakes, cigarettes are smoked, one after another. We repeat
the same things, the same gestures, all we can manage is to renew
this sameness. Two hours ago strangers came between us and didn't
leave until the train left. They didn't leave, they stayed, I left. Among

strangers, we grew even stranger to each other. Smiles were exchanged, then handshakes, cigarettes were smoked. I was disgusted. We didn't part, they separated us. They were filled with joy. No one felt jealous of anyone else. I felt jealous.

In the spring weather, train windows remain open. The wind carries death inside. The new death, the one to be renewed. I must die in the blue of spring.

1954

# THE ZANZALAK TREE

What is called a heartache
is but a *zanzalak* tree
under the *zanzalak* tree
your shadows stand, but not you
— *Saffet N. Sener*

What is being described here? Perhaps Riza. Rather, the way he used to be before Demir arrived from Ankara. I understand it tonight. It could have been love, but was not. He knocked on my door three hours ago. He hadn't done that for months; I hadn't realized until then. I don't even recall if I told him to come in. First, he peered through the door. I think his demeanor reminded me of his reticence in the early days. The food is ready, he said, and entered the room. I wondered where his mother was. I'm coming, I said. If his mother had been home, she wouldn't have let anybody else call me for dinner. You two should start, I think I said, I'll be there as soon as I finish addressing this envelope. He didn't leave. There's nobody but us for dinner, he said. I should undress. It's cold, I can't stay in these clothes, I have to take them off. I was surprised. Where is your mother? I asked. She's seeing Demir off. I had forgotten. She would be spending the night in Pendik. I should go to bed, what's the use of staying up in this cold? I addressed the envelope. It was twelve past eight. He turned off the light in the room. I walked behind him as we went to the dining room. He had cunning written on the back of his neck. A tense neck, like the tall back of a chair. The cold numbs the mind, I am freezing. The table . . . I'm finished undressing now. The table had been opened. I laughed. Why did you open it just for the two of us? A bed is always cold when one is alone. So much for the radiator. This room is even colder than the outermost room in a house with a woodstove. Yes, he said, just for the two of us. My mind is starting to warm up. Just the two of us, he said. So what if I opened the table? We can each sit at one end. I should stretch out my legs, but it's impossible between these icy sheets. We can talk across the table for a change. He meant, We need distance. Before Demir, we used to sit at the three sides of the table, his mother to my right, he to my left. The water pitcher, the bread basket, and the saltshaker would be lined up along the fourth side. I stretch, I have to resist pulling my knees up to my belly until the bed gets warm. My feet were far from his. He used to rest his feet near mine. They were never still, though. He used to shake his leg. Tonight he meant, We should keep some distance. We sat. When Demir was around, he stopped shaking his leg. He was stiff as stone for a week. Tonight he sat in Demir's chair, away from me. A soft noise is coming through the window. Snow must have piled up. I'll check it in a little while. The wind must be blowing in Pendik too, cold, bitter. His mother would be cold. Is he cold, too? We sat at the two ends of the long cold table we sat without speaking a word ate in silence forgot to eat in silence looked at each other caught each other's eyes lowered our heads and looked back at our plates pretended we were eating and still looked at each other. The snow is piling high against the window, flake by flake, soft. It spills, like specks of dust, crisp, unhurried, mounding down below, dirty. Just when I had gotten warm, I'm cold again. As if I *had* to look out the window. We were staring at each other. But I soon stopped. His faraway face was tiring. Demir must have reached Bilecik by now. His mother must be asleep in Pendik. And he . . . Was he jealous of Demir? I couldn't understand. His own brother.

    I hadn't seen him the day he arrived. We introduced ourselves the next day. Light brown hair, yellowish-brown. His eyes pale green like Riza's eyes. But Riza's seemed paler, much paler against his dark skin. I stopped looking at his eyes while we ate. I stuffed my belly. Stubbornly. When he asked if I wanted a tangerine, I said no and didn't even raise my head. He was quiet. Demir was always talkative. Even that first evening when he sat next to me. Told me all about Ankara, his father, what he did in school. His face in an endless smile. His eyes the laughing kind. If Riza was jealous, what was he jealous of? Was it because I showed interest? He finally made it clear tonight. He knows perfectly well that there is no reason to be jealous. He should know. He ought to have known. Whatever happened had happened in four days, Demir and I had said our farewells last night. Vacation was over, he had to return to Ankara. He had acted as if he didn't know his brother or mother. Obviously he loves his father more, prefers the house there. He had spoken only with me. Big, overgrown, animal child. He went to bed early, thinking he wouldn't be able to sleep. His mother had also remained aloof. Something else is possible. Riza might have bad-mouthed me. Then I will move out. They had gone to bed after-ward. I won't look out the window again. What's there to see anyway? Folds and folds of snow, the hill is entirely covered, the sounds of streetcars and automobiles are smothered, as if coming from three streets down. I can't fall asleep. I'm not sleepy. The bed is finally warm. Probably Riza isn't asleep either. He probably hasn't even warmed up yet. Cold air seeps through his window. Especially on windy nights like this. If Demir is still troubling his mind, Demir is gone. His mother loves Demir; even if she doesn't love him as much as she loves Riza, she still loves him, I know. Riza ought to know this, too. As he once told me, he has grown accustomed to his mother seeing Demir only twice a year, for the past twelve years. He tolerates sharing her love for four, five days, without complaint. The blanket feels less and less heavy. My body must have been tense when I first laid down. The bed is warm but I should still bundle up. A fine day the radiator picked to break down. Instead of eating a tangerine, I lit a cigarette. He cleared the table while I warmed my hands over the gas stove. He pushed the table's leaves shut with a loud bang. Suddenly the room grew larger. In the middle stood the table, forlorn, the old familiar table where the three of us used to sit — the pitcher, the bread basket, the saltshaker lined up along the fourth side — his mother to my right, he to my left, his leg incessantly shaking underneath. The distance between us disappeared. Still, I didn't look at his face. As though I knew that if I looked, his eyes would be pleading. But it wasn't because I knew. Rather, because I was afraid that I would think that his eyes were pleading. If the snow ever stops, I'll sleep. A wide spacious sleep inside a white rumbling noise.

If only my wrists would stop aching. The clock ticks on the table. Riza must have fallen asleep. From his lit window — the glass panes broken — the melting snow falls five stories down, thump after dull thump. Hitting the ground, it fans out like scarves. So he was able to sleep. Turning his back against the noise, ignoring it. Is he finally calm? Maybe, even in sleep, he is still jealous of Demir — whatever Demir means to him.

When he was walking beside that girl a few days ago in Beyoğlu, he must have seen me. Otherwise, he wouldn't have hung on to her arm so clumsily, so tastelessly. Ugly Riza. Ugly in his beauty. How could this be love? He's afraid. Afraid of his brother. Afraid of me. Love should be fearless. Especially if it is difficult. Who was that girl? Probably his friend. From school maybe. Who knows what time it is? The cold is smothered by the silence. He and the girl were walking side by side. When our eyes met—the way I saw it—he tried to look away but failed, his hand searched for the girl's arm, his blind hand, his inexperienced hand, he blushed by the time he found the arm, then he put his hand on her arm and pulled the girl against him. I walked by. From the corner of my eye, I saw his eyes still searching for mine. Did he want to show that he had feelings, that he could feel? I already believed he could. Yet that day shattered my belief. He cannot feel. Much less love. He used that girl. He was jealous of Demir. He is all the more guilty for that. He must be asleep by now. Still a child. He wanted to be cross with me tonight. Couldn't even succeed in that. The trees must be heavy with snow. I must tell him about the *zanzalak* tree. Large, heavy, tall, its fruit delicious, most delicious, said the poet. Its shade wide, dark, deep, warm. The bed is warm now. I feel the cold in my head, my stiff forehead. The shade of the *zanzalak* tree must be warm. I have to describe to him the fruit as I know it. As soon as you grab it, you want to bite into it, said the poet. It must be like Riza. You bite into it, yes, but you can't figure out why it's tasteless. Love overwhelms you. I need blood to bind me. As it flows—it must flow through the bite, the blood dripping hot—as it flows, it binds. Death, I need my death. No, it can't be like Riza. That tasteless fruit doesn't know blood, can't recognize it. He has no blood. Under the *zanzalak* tree, your shadows stand, not you, said Saffet. Your death. If I am to die, what better death than one under the *zanzalak* tree? But it won't be. Death simply is. Mine is a carcass. Riza can't be love. He was afraid. I must move out of this house. Is he afraid in his sleep, too? In sleep he can no longer have his friend his friendship his passion his fear he can no longer yearn

for elsewhere or hesitate or feel jealous. Demir is far away mother-
less alone with his own strength he is scared ruined dead I don't
regret I don't regret that I loved he's not the only one ruined and
what of it he will burn and in burning his taste will ripen what love
is must burst its skin must open itself to the sun and bleed I can't
believe it's hard to believe this cowardly tastelessness this love like
cold snow is what is being described

1954

# SCORCHED

At first, I noticed the pitch-dark sky, then, the streaks of rain on the glass. The room was dark. My father was getting dressed; I had to get up. At the foot of my bed was a basket of clothes. A mound of clothes, bigger than the ones I've seen on washdays, ironed, unironed, all jumbled together. I looked at my father; Get up, he said. He had put on his jacket. I couldn't ask what had happened. Then he put on his raincoat. There was a fire, he said, you didn't hear. I was shocked. I don't believe it, I said. Look out the window, he said. Walking toward the window, I asked, Where? First Haluk Bey's house burned, then Rahmi Bey's, came my father's voice. A fire hose stretched in front of our door. The stones were all muddied. I saw Fikret under the window. He was waving his arms and hands. I could hear the rumble of a crowd on the street, but Fikret's voice was muffled. I can't remember how I opened the window. "The whole village was awake and you slept through it," Fikret said. "Come down so we go and see Blind Meryem." I ran to the back door. The roofs of the two houses had collapsed; rafters, charred and bare, rose-hued, reached toward the sky. I put on my clothes. As I was running down the stairs, Mother grabbed me. "Nazmiye Hanim and her children are downstairs. We took them in and whatever they could rescue. Behave yourself." She hugged me, then gave me a kiss. Three huge bundles of clothes sat at the bottom of the stairway. The air started to smell burned. Aunt Nazmiye's eyes were full of tears. Nermin and Nazmi stood like strangers in the hall. I kissed Aunt Nazmiye's hand and tried to say something appropriate, I think. She pulled me to her bosom and kissed me. The air smelled like charcoal kept in buckets. I looked at Nermin and Nazmi but didn't know what to say. They avoided my eyes, anyway. I lowered my head, and looking down, I walked out. Mother didn't make me eat breakfast, I realized, and was puzzled. I saw my father in the distance, coming from the meadow to the station road. I hadn't seen him leave the house. Suddenly Fikret materialized in front of me. He looked inside the house and whispered, "They're still with you; if your mother hadn't taken them in, they'd be left out on the street. We don't have room, you know. Your house is bigger. Hasan Bey also arrived just now. He keeps looking at Nazmiye Hanim's house, dumbfounded. Come on, let's go and see Blind Meryem." We started walking. The stones had begun to dry. The fire hose was pulled back; it suddenly disappeared. The grass was vibrant green, glowing, clean. Dead-nettle odor mixed in with the charcoal smell. A thick, heavy smell. A hot, pungent, congealed smell. The sky was pitch dark. The air smelled like blood. Even the sky. It was like the smell in the pharmacy on the day when Nebilé fell off her bicycle. Dark blood on her dark skin, smelling just like this. Smell of flesh, bloody, burned-flesh smell. The sky was pitch dark. When did it rain? I asked. "It started raining when they put out the fire. I can't believe that you slept through it all." We turned the corner and took the crowded, wet street. Fikret nudged me. "Look at Hasan Bey. Were you really not awakened?" No, I said. "You must be one heavy sleeper. Fire trucks rushed here all the way from Demirli. All of Sarikum shook and trembled with the noise of water pumps, and you heard nothing. You're kidding, right?" Hasan Bey was upset. We walked toward him. "I woke up at three. It was totally dark. My mother was talking with my dad in the yard. My sister was getting dressed. Then I noticed the glow beyond the yard. Granny came down the stairs, turned on the lights, and announced that the fire had spread to Aunt Nazmiye's house. My sister rushed out to the yard, and we followed. Your mom and dad were in your yard, talking to my parents. I asked about you. They said you were sleeping. Granny advised your mom to gather everything; if the fire moved this way, we'd be ruined, our whole row would also burn. The village fire engine arrived then. Flames were shooting up behind Nazmi's roof, but then we realized it was Haluk Bey's home that was ablaze. There was a sudden flare. Your father and mine rushed to help. Granny came to your house. Your father apparently told them not to wake you up. He and your mom gathered up the clothes while you were still asleep."

I didn't believe him. "And you didn't wake up?" I stared at his face. No, I said, and then? "Well, then, we also gathered up what we could. They brought your bags down to the first floor. Granny returned. She and my mom got dressed and left. That's when they saw Aunt Nazmiye, her children, and her two bags sitting on the sidewalk. Your dad, our folks took them to your place. Even our Zehra was awakened, kept crying till morning. How come you slept through it all!" Then we listened to Hasan Bey. He spoke breathlessly, "They burned down my house. They burned down my house. I wish she were dead, forgive me, God, as if their iniquity weren't enough, they also burned down my house. Dear God, look, have pity on your poor Hasan! Take her life so no one should call her Çuhaci's daughter any more. I have no honor left." People tried to calm him, but they were laughing behind his back. Someone said, "Uncle Hasan has gone crazy for good." "They burned down my house, the damned lot!" Hasan Bey kept saying. Fikret pulled me by the arm. "Come on, let's check out Blind Meryem." Where's Uncle Rahmi? I asked. "He should be here soon; Dad phoned him right away. Turns out he was in Istanbul. Aunt Nazmiye is waiting for him to come back so they can pack what's left and go to Istanbul. Come on, let's check out Meryem." I was thinking of Fikret's dad. It must be nice to be the station chief and talk on the phone with Istanbul. My father also talks on the phone, but only when he's in Istanbul. I don't know if he ever has here. When we walked past Haluk Bey's house, only the four walls were still standing. Through the windows we saw the soot-blackened plaster fallen between the large posts. Where is Haluk Bey then? I asked. "He was sleeping at the time. They barely managed to wake him in time and rescue him. The entire back of the house was on fire. The house was already almost gone. Whatever they tried didn't help much. He couldn't salvage much. His books, everything burned." The books had no pictures anyway, I had leafed through them one day. "What he could save he put in a suitcase, mumbled something, then left for Istanbul, I think. Early this morning. The firemen tried hard to save Hasan Bey's house. The upper floor is gone but the lower floor is still in place. Come on, now you'll see Meryem." The smell of burnt flesh mixed in with the smell of charcoal, then dispersed. We walked toward the gardens. Now it smelled of burned grass. Fikret reached up and picked two peaches from a branch, bit into one, gave me the other. He laughed mockingly. "You're still sleeping. Where do you think we're going?" I don't know, I said. To Meryem's garden, right? And why are we going to see Meryem? She'd chase us away again. Fikret was laughing; he pulled me along. The garden gate was open. We entered; the dogs didn't bark. The water in the cistern was bright green, mossy, as always, thick on the edges. The leaves falling from the trees snuggled up next to one another like lambs. Fikret again pulled me by my shoulder. We had reached the rows of corn. We dove in; we were nearing the site of the fire. Walking between the plants, we came to the plot behind the houses. From here, they looked more burned, starkly outlined. Right behind the houses, a crowd had gathered, with heads lowered, looking at the ground. Tall policemen were walking around. What's happening? I said, Where's Meryem? We retreated back to where we'd been. "The police won't let us in from the other end, we can approach this way." To whom? The heads in the crowd turned toward us. "Shut up, silly," Fikret said, "they'll chase us out." I shut up. We slipped through the legs, hips. I stretched my head to see. "There is Blind Meryem," Fikret said. On the ground, completely charred, was a form vaguely resembling a human. Then, I could discern a woman's body. Her legs were bent, her knees next to her head. Swollen like a bag. But her head, her face, I couldn't make out. I began to discern her arms, her back, her butt, her thighs, one by one. Blind Meryem had been burned in the fire. This was Meryem. Suddenly, the odor became noticeable. The odor of Meryem's dark, charred, torn flesh was rising to the sky. The wounds were bright red, bloody. Her charred skin was cracked like famished soil, like the soil around the lighthouse.

I waited for a wave to come, just as I did by the lighthouse, for the blood to form a lake, a sea, and carry away the cracks. The smell of flesh covered everything. Suddenly Nebilé appeared beside me. I looked at her. Her mouth agape, her chin dropped, she was staring at Meryem. Then, I heard her slight, muted voice say, "Oh God, now she looks like me." I remembered Meryem chasing Nebilé away, calling her "filthy Arab." Meryem's pitch-black body was laying in a green coffin, a yellow coffin. Her perfectly round head, bald, its skin lacerated. Afterward, I noticed an old, blackened rosy hue on the soles of her feet. Then everyone started talking all at once. Through the noise, two policemen's hands holding a sack reached out and covered Meryem's body. Why are they covering her? I asked Fikret. Then the crowd of legs and hips parted. We were thrown out, drowning in the noise. They were laughing, shouting. I ran. When I stopped, the Çuhaci house stood in front of me. I had even run past the mulberry tree that stood in the middle of the meadow. Fikret caught up with me. Mushfik was with him. And behind him, his dogs. I sat on the ground. There was no sound coming from the Çuhacis' twelve-room mansion. The entire village was swarming around Meryem's body lying behind the houses past the road, past the meadow. The two boys sat on each side of me, and the dogs lay on the grass across from us. Tails, ears, muffled voices, big eyes, they howled softly and let their heads fall between their feet. "Couldn't keep your mouth shut, could you?" said Mushfik. Fikret added, "They chased us out because of you." Then they remained silent; so did I. What would you have seen? I said later. They didn't respond. Mushfik opened his mouth, folded his upper lip in, clenched his teeth, moved his temples, and finally said, "It was horrible, disgusting. But I still would've looked. Soon they'll come and take her away." "And we won't get to see her anymore," added Fikret, "how would we?" How did Meryem burn? I asked. Then the odor reached our nostrils. The dry, yellow weeds couldn't have smelled. I realized a wind had started blowing. The odor of charcoal and flesh spread throughout Sarikum. "I know," Mushfik said. "So do I," Fikret chimed in. "You can't know better than me; my father told me." Fikret fell silent. "Last night, he was returning from the old district. He'd gone to Arif's. You know Arif, the fisherman who lives on the point, near the cemetery. The one who sells lobsters on Sunday mornings to the mansions along the asphalt road. Dad had gone to visit him. On the way back, he thought of taking the shortcut around Meryem's garden, and that's when he saw. In the plot behind the houses, right in front of the rows of corn, Meryem was sitting with four or five men, drinking *raki*. Also with them was that Zehra, the wh-h-hore Zehra. They were all totally drunk. They weren't making too much noise, but they were giggling. Then they kissed and hugged, rolling on the ground, one on top of the other!" "Did your father tell you all that?" asked Fikret. "You're making it up. How can you know?" Mushfik breathed heavily. "Fine! I made it up. My dad didn't tell me. I know. You know." Go on, Mushfik, I think I said. "Then, my dad said, they were laughing, speaking in whispers. They had candles with them. My dad walked behind the garden and the houses and made it to the road. Everyone was asleep. He thought of knocking on their doors, telling them in the houses, but changed his mind. He entered our yard through the back gate, of course, the gate near the plum trees. He put the lock on and locked it. So that the drunks couldn't get into our yard. Then he saw the men getting up, taking Zehra along with them, and walking down the road. When he was convinced they were far away, he gave a sigh of relief and went in the house. I heard him come in. I'm a light sleeper." What about Meryem? I said. "Well, here is what happened. She must have passed out when her friends left. Remember the candles, they must have started the grass on fire. Meryem burned, so did the houses." Well, didn't she scream when burning?

"I told you. She had passed out. I know, Dad passes out sometimes. My mom says so, He passed out, she says. Then she tries to undress him, put him to bed, can't carry him, shakes him but can't wake him up." Why does your dad pass out, I asked. "Why else, when you drink *raki*, you pass out." My dad drinks, too, I said, but he doesn't pass out. "He doesn't drink much, that's why. Mine, when he drinks he drinks a lot." *Raki* stinks, Mushfik. Like medicine. Like the stinky stuff they made me drink when we first arrived here. It smells like that. How can they drink it? "How would I know, maybe the grown-ups like it . . . or maybe . . ." So Meryem drank *raki* and passed out. You think she was in pain? "No doubt about it," said Fikret, "I burned my finger the other day. I know. It hurts a lot." "But we said she passed out, Fikret. Supposedly, when you pass out, you're like dead, you feel nothing. Besides, the burning grass must have first torched her dress, then her hair. She must have fainted from the heat. Anyway, if she was in pain, serves her right!" "Shame on you," Fikret interrupted, "she is dead!" It's a sin, Mushfik, I said. Mushfik snickered, "So drinking's not a sin? I was disgusted, disgusted but I still would have looked." Look, I said. Hasan Bey of the Çuhaci family was coming.

Two people walked beside him, holding Hasan Bey up by his armpits. When he got near us, the dogs leaped up, growling. Mushfik hit Barut on the head. Defeated, both dogs laid down by our feet. Hasan Bey walked past us. We continued to stare. He shook the others off in front of his garden gate; they quickly left him. He turned, facing the other end of the meadow. "Cursed ones!" he shouted, spat on the ground, pushed the gate open, and entered. Just when we lost sight of him among the trees, a train slowly passed by the house. All five of us were startled by the sound of the train. Confused, we watched it pass. Then I felt my head getting warm. The clouds had parted a little. The sun was shining above us. I was hungry. Let's go, I said. We got up. As we passed under the mulberry tree, Fikret said, "The crowd looks smaller"; we walked. My mother and Fikret's mother were calling us, waving their hands. As we got closer, I heard their scolding words. It was well past mealtime, they said. Musfhik said, "My mom must be waiting," and left. I saw Reshit Efendi coming from the site of the fire. The dogs walked toward Reshit Efendi. I understood that Mushfik didn't want his father to see him. He took off running. We stayed. A car stopped in front of the plot. The men were carrying a heavy sack. When they loaded it in the car, I saw the two charred legs dangling out of the sack. Fikret and I ran. They held us back. As the car drove off, Meryem's legs, her dark, pitch-black, blood-red, scarred legs were dangling, dangling.

Nazmi and her family had left the house. My mother held and kissed me. "Nazmiye made me promise. She wanted to kiss you before she left. Obviously, she couldn't. Where have you been?" We went to see Meryem, I said, thinking about the coldness in her kiss. I realized later, the kiss was not from her but from Aunt Nazmiye. And then she began her scolding. She yelled, "Answer me! What business did you have going to see Meryem! Answer me!" I couldn't. She grabbed my arm and dragged me to the sink. I go to the sink regularly and wash my hands; I do it before every meal anyway. This time she washed my hands. Soon after we were seated at the table, my father arrived. We remembered then that it was Saturday. We waited for him. He sat, and we started eating. Then he spoke, "I talked with Rahmi Bey at the station. Hope they have a safe trip." Morsels came between his words. "The worst is, the children were terrified, I feel sorry for them. They still looked confused, those bright kids." I didn't say a word about having found Nermin's handkerchief with bears and deer on it. It was tucked in a corner of the sofa. "And you know what I learned from the police chief?" He lowered his voice. I didn't raise my head. Trying to hear, I kept eating my food. "You know the story Reshit Efendi told. Well, the worst of it happened after Meryem was left alone. Rahmi Bey told me at the station. He apparently heard it from Nazmiye Hanim. The poor woman couldn't bring herself to tell us what she had seen. As it turns out, she woke up sometime in the night, and when she saw light coming through the back window, she decided to take a look; in the light of a single candle, Meryem was totally naked on the grass." "Was there anyone with her?" my mother asked, whispering. My father lowered his voice even further. "No, not at all, alone, she was alone; quivering on the grass, her body assuming strange shapes." I froze. His voice was nearly inaudible. "Ill . . . poisoned . . . she thought . . . but she wasn't ill . . . you understand . . ." he said and paused. From his hands, I understood he was looking at me. I tried not to raise my head. I kept eating without interruption. "Then?" asked my mother. I looked at her, then at my father. "Then she went back to bed. Thinking Meryem would get up once she felt fine. Didn't think much of it, even though she'd seen the candle. She was drowsy to begin with, so she went back to sleep. They were full of remorse, both of them, while telling me all this. Nazmiye Hanim kept wishing she hadn't gone back to sleep, while Rahmi Bey wished she had woken someone up and told them what she'd seen. Who could I have woken? Nazmiye Hanim asked. I kept quiet. So did Rahmi. Thank god, nobody knew about Hasan Bey, otherwise . . . it would have been bad. Rahmi's eyes filled with tears, I swear . . . Anyway . . . The police chief knew more . . . How about you go upstairs, your mother and I have to talk." Just below my face was his finger motioning me to go. His finger briefly stopped at my plate. It was full of medlar seeds. I was surprised. I left the table. They closed the door behind me. I sat by the door. There was a slight tapping on the front door. Fikret had come. I let him in, told him to be quiet, and went back to the dining room door. "They got her drunk and left her," my father was saying inside. "I gather, they were caught and interrogated. The strange thing is, they didn't even try to deny any of it." My mother whispered something. "I don't know. She must have passed out completely. The candle melted entirely, of course. Set the grass on fire, then her. The grocer said that Meryem had bought ten candles the day before." Then I heard my father getting up. I ran away from the door. Fikret and I went out in the street. We walked without saying a word. Under the sun, the breezeless sky turned a sharper shade of blue; it hurt my eyes and scarred my eyelids; we kept walking along the edge of the road covered with patches of mostly dried grass, passing the cats and the sprouts of stinky weeds by the walls. The wooden facades felt hot, they could have flared up any time, and the hot stones could have cracked open like loaves of bread in hot stone ovens. In the sweltering heat, Mushfik's home smelled like a crack in the earth. Cool, musty. Dilaver Hanim was sitting at the window, ruffling Mushfik's hair as he sat next to her, reading a book. She gathered herself at once. "Welcome," she said. Mushfik raised his head from his book; his face flushed red. The same shade of red we were used to seeing when we caught him doing something other than what we thought he was doing, or when he came up with strange questions out of nowhere while doing his homework. His eyes were wide open. I didn't ask anything then. Both of us peered through the window. "Don't come in," Mushfik said in a muffled voice. "I'm coming out." I asked what he was reading. Dilaver Hanim, pulled out of her lethargy, said to him, "Why won't you let them come inside? Why go out in this heat?" Mushfik didn't even look at her. *"Monkey's Hand,"* he said, then came outside. Dilaver Hanim spoke again with much difficulty: "Your mother, your granny, how are they?" Granny had been in Istanbul for three days, would probably be returning the day after tomorrow, I said. "Give them my regards. Would love to come and visit, but . . ." Dilaver Hanim slipped back into her own thoughts. Mushfik pulled me by the arm. "Let's go," he said. We walked toward the sea, alongside the mansions. I asked him why he had blushed when he saw us. He whispered in my ear, "My mother's hand was in my hair, that's why." I was surprised; we didn't talk any more. Rambling, we reached the first wheat field. Stepping on the stubby, hard stalks, feeling their nakedness—bare, cracked, burned, blackened nakedness—we reached the naked road. Then we descended to the sea. The sea was naked also. In the distance, far away, a few broken waves were curving, pure white. The sea was utterly calm. The lighthouse on the left, tall, solitary in its whiteness between the yellow and the calm, deep, rich blue-green. On the right, in the distance where Sarikum extends a narrow arm into the sea, I thought I saw, in the shimmering light, the windows of Arif's house. Then we heard something like thunder. I was looking at Fikret. We both turned to look at Mushfik. As always, he was skipping stones. This time, I found it strange, we didn't speak at all. It was strange. We remained quiet.

Later, Mushfik spoke, as if reading from a book, "Meryem was a sinful woman. My mother said so. She was a whore . . ."

. I felt nauseous .

". . . She'll burn in hell, my mother said . . ."

. I wanted to throw up. in Meryem's rose-hued scorched brokenness, there was no place for hell fires. no place left .

". . . They'll burn her flesh. Shove a red-hot iron in her thing . . ."

. have shame, Fikret said. shame Mushfik .

". . . Shame is climbing on top of each other in the garden, like dogs, not like cats or birds, like dogs . . ."

. we fell silent, surrounded by the murmur of the waves .

". . . Like dogs, they were rolling on the ground, kneeling, I saw them one day, I saw, among the corn, first the man stood in front of her, Meryem was laughing, as if tickled . . ."

. the waves grew louder .

". . . I was hiding. He untied his pants, let them drop, I saw Meryem's legs, then her butt, when he climbed on her, Meryem giggled, then screamed, he was a big man, then, like dogs, they moved back and forth . . ."

. the waves' spray amid the roaring. I tensed up .

". . . Then they fell on the ground, crushing the blades of grass, the green covering their bodies, then his legs stretched, stretched, stretched . . ."

. Mushfik was screaming. drowned out by the waves. he tossed the pebbles. we got splashed. by the lighthouse .

". . . Then drew back . . ."

then the roar died down. The waves receded. Mushfik squatted on the ground. The smaller pebbles floated on the sea's surface. In the distance, a ship turned the point in front of Arif's house and the old district; it disappeared in the light, without even leaving a shadow. At the foot of the lighthouse, water would be dripping down the rocks, into the sea.

After the huge crashing wave, smaller ones followed. Blinded by the light, I could barely make out the white lighthouse. Let's go back, I think I said. I didn't understand much of Mushfik's description, but I did sense I wasn't supposed to ask any questions. Later, I whispered in Mushfik's ear, How come your mother knows that Meryem is a bad person? "Why wouldn't she? Of course she knows." And why were you upset that she was caressing your hair? "I keep telling her I don't love her. She loves me, but she's often hurtful. That's why I don't love her." Don't you ever kiss her? "Of course I do. Every morning and every night. Then she scolds me, then I'm cross, then we make up. But she's hurtful. I don't like that. That's why, when she was caressing my hair in front of you—" Fikret asked suddenly, "What are you two whispering about?" I looked at Mushfik again. How about Uncle Reshit, is he hurtful to you? Every time I bought *böreks* and pastries from him, he'd ask me about my father and mother, so I thought of him as considerate. My mother keeps telling me, considerate people are good people. "No, he's not," Mushfik said. "He's not hurtful, ever, but neither does he love me. It's obvious he doesn't. He treats me like I'm a stranger. I try to be proud of him sometimes. But it doesn't work, I know he doesn't love me. He breaks my spirit. I'd almost say I'm not his son . . ." Then he was lost in his thoughts. I liked Uncle Reshit. That is, I used to like him. But after what Mushfik said, I would not love, I would never love Uncle Reshit. How could he not love Mushfik? At first, I didn't believe it, couldn't believe it. How can he not love you? I asked Mushfik. Then he swore he didn't. "I'm not lying," he said. Then I knew he was telling the truth. Fikret was walking ahead of us. We caught up with him. When we got to the asphalt road, we saw my father coming toward us, together with Suat's father. I left the boys and ran to him. I held my father's hand. I held it tightly. He did, too, I think. Uncle Hasan didn't notice me. He was telling my father, "He has aged, grown senile, too. Father is decrepit as much as his brother Ali is strong and sharp. Since this morning, he has said nothing but 'they burned down my house.' As if my brother's sorrow wasn't enough, as if it wasn't enough to feel sorry for all the burned houses *and* for the burned woman . . . Having to listen to his rambling . . . I love Rahmi like a brother. But because of Father, I get to see neither him nor Nazmiye as much as I would like to. And weren't we there, watching the fire? I swear, he stood in front of the door and said, 'If you try to help them, may you see me dead.' The house that's in flames is his own daughter's house, Rahmi's house, those inside are his own daughter and grandchildren; he even knows Rahmi is away in Istanbul for two days. The house that's burning is his own house, my friend! And still . . . I thought I'd go insane watching him. Then, you should've seen Huseyin. He's my brother and I wouldn't want to criticize him, I wouldn't, but his is yet another sort of oddness. He takes after my uncle. All he cares about is to be commissioned so he can rebuild Sarikum to his own liking, after his own fancy. It wouldn't surprise me if he attempts to do it one of these days. You won't believe it, but for a moment he almost seemed happy. 'Look,' he said, 'in place of those houses, more beautiful ones can be built; besides, they were the ugliest houses in Sarikum.' Then he added, 'I'm sure our folks managed to save their lives,' when he noticed the way my father was looking at him. I knew, of course, why my father was looking at him like that. Because you know, as long as a house belongs to Hasan Çuhaci, it is beautiful, even if it looks like a run-down hut. How can something belong to Hasan Çuhaci and not be beautiful; worse yet, how can you call it ugly? Is it conceivable? Already this morning, even before we were out on the street, can you believe what Huseyin told me? He grabbed me by the shoulder, 'Imagine,' he said, 'beautiful new houses.' Can you believe, in this entire family, not one person dared to ask if Nazmiye was all right, after hearing my father's words? Except for Nimet, she kept thinking about her all night long, I know she did, but she didn't say a word even to me. Suat loves his aunt, you know. When he saw we could do nothing, the boy was heartbroken, I swear . . ."

We walked silently for some time. A little later, Uncle Hasan asked me, "How are you?" Fine, I said, but he didn't hear. We were nearing the station. When we got there, he left us. We watched him go. Soon I couldn't see his head. I slowly pulled on my father's hand. A train passed the station, then the blueness of the sky melted on the horizon and the station lights came on. Under the diminishing blue, we headed home, slowly letting the darkness close in. A kind of grief was in the air. An unbroken silence. Inside this silence we passed from the pavement to the meadow, from the meadow to the road leading to our house. My mother was at the door, waiting for us. "I was worried," she said in the distance. When we didn't respond, she asked, "Did he do something wrong?" My father replied, "No." The table was set. Suddenly, I was overcome with exhaustion. Father was telling Mother something as she went into the kitchen. I stood in the corner, leaned against the wall, and did not move. A while later Mother came to me. The air smelled of flowers, it smelled burned, it smelled of flesh, it was hot, Mother took me to the sink, washed my hands and face, hurt me while she dried them, I said nothing, Father came, he had changed his clothes, he said he wished he had a radio tonight, we sat at the table, had beans cooked in olive oil, *koftes*, salad, rice, Fikret called me from the open window, he was just returning home, Mother told him, he can't come, he is eating now, the door to Fikret's house opened, closed, Zehra began crying, her granny sang her a lullaby, Fikret tapped on the wall three times, I tapped back, they're eating too, my father said, Hasan Bey must still be spewing curses at his daughter, Mother said, I hope poor Nazmiye can at least get a peaceful sleep tonight, where did Rahmi Bey take them, I wonder, Father replied, Rahmi talked about renting a place but tonight they'd be in a hotel, where else could he take them, Mother spoke, full of grief, she had a house until yesterday and today she has nowhere to go, let Hasan Bey think about the house, Father responded, poor girl, Mother said, what kind of a father is he, Mother pushed the rice toward me, has he no heart, still mad at his daughter, won't help her even in time of disaster, not even her brothers went to rescue her, how could they, Father asked, how could they, he stood in front of the door and forbade them, may you see me dead if you go, he told them, heartless man, Mother said, he's willing to let his own house burn down, all this hatred against Rahmi, why, he provides for his family just fine, I've never heard of him disappointing Nazmiye even once, you know how much they love each other, and their kids, I bet they're much better off than all the kids living in their grandfather's home, except for Suat, I thought, I love Suat a lot, Mushfik loves him too, but I said nothing to my mother, Father said, Suat is the only good one among them, true, the kid's mother couldn't win over any hearts among the Çuhacis nor the whole pack of their relatives, but she never refuses Hasan Bey's wishes, I'm especially concerned about his son, Hasan, he is sick, you know, God forbid, if something happened to him, both Nimet and Suat would be ruined, Hasan Bey wants his son by his side, but if something happens, he'll kick them both out, Mother said, I swear, he complained when his son took an outsider but accepted the woman as long as they agreed to live with him and instead of helping out his daughter he rejected her because she married Rahmi as if he could find a better son-in-law among the Çuhaci clan but no Rahmi Bey had even agreed to live with them and Hasan Bey still rejected them I'm amazed he let them have that house of his and what is he left with now besides his meanness and if Nazmiye ever returns here she'd be stupid — then I get to keep Nermin's handkerchief, I thought to myself — let them be for God's sake my father said look at your son he said he is falling asleep

Mother said finish your grapes I am not falling asleep I am listening I wanted to say but didn't I ate my grapes Father said Nazmiye then Hasan Bey he said then go get undressed Mother said seeing Meryem she said Meryem was stark naked stark naked naked naked

My head on the plate of grapes, I fell asleep. They told me so this morning. Meryem won't leave my sight, scorched . . . At first, I noticed the pitch-dark sky.

1954

# FORK

*No me acuerdo quien fui*
*no me acuerdo quien soy,*
*ni de donde partí*
*ni hacia donde me voy.*

*Fuéronseme a perder*
*raices de verdad,*
*que he perdido la fe*
*en mi immortalidad . . .*

—Miguel de Unamuno, *Cancionero*

## I

Inside the sun-cracked shell of the house, the silence felt heavy, pregnant. In the dark, damp coolness of the ivy path leading to the back door, a muted sense of longing touched my wet skin. I thought I would probably never see Suat again; the nights that would pass without Suat, without the sea. I thought that I would never kiss him again. I remember the same dark green coolness pouring through another sweltering day like this years ago, when I hugged and kissed Suat in the middle of our games and saw his great-grandmother approaching us from the back door. I stood still once again as I had that day. I could feel the weight of Suat's body in my lap. But today no door opened. That day I had kept repeating to Suat, "The grand matron, your great-grandmother is coming, she saw us, she is coming." "Don't worry," he replied, "she won't understand a thing even if she sees us, don't you know she's crazy?" She had been standing in the middle of the ivy path. We had stiffened, standing on the threshold of darkness and heat. The grand matron's lips were moving. I could still hear her yelling, "Shameless." Silence crackling in the dark. "Shameless green cows the sea blue I said Efendi the milky grass inside they are flirting," I could still hear her saying. Then, her eyes staring not at us but at some distant point, she had passed through the ivy into the sweltering heat, her giant body diminishing like a tiny fly in the dense foliage. Suat's hair was sweaty. "She is crazy, but I still got scared for a minute. That she'd see us." Today the path was vacant. Except for my damp skin, nothing was alive. *I knew* I wouldn't find Suat at home. *I knew* he wouldn't want to see me after yesterday. I tapped on the door.

Silence swallowed the tapping; hearts pulsed in the dark emptiness. The pattering sounds would not cease, the pattering of years. I pressed my palm against the door, tapped it again with my fingers. Then I realized the door was unlocked. It opened without squeaking. Forcing myself through the pattering, I walked toward the stairs. Suddenly, from the upstairs window near the ceiling, a beam of sunlight streamed over me. Darkness dispersed in the murmur that replaced the pattering. The sound of light shimmering over my body echoed in the distance, in the cool desolation outlined by doorways. I ascended through the stream of light without making the steps squeak.

By the time I reached the top of the stairway, I no longer remembered the sweltering heat, the green and the darkness. I relaxed, moved away first from the light, then from the silence. The door to Suat's room was ajar. I walked with senseless hope. The Çuhaci family's empty house suddenly began rumbling. I slowly pushed the door open.

A hinge creaked briefly and stopped. The furniture was bathed in sunlight but nowhere could I see Suat. I'll always remember this room in sunlight. I can't picture this room growing dark, night ever returning. I can't imagine a green moon streaming through the window. Perhaps I will never see the room the way it was. Perhaps he was right that night . . .

## II

Few days remained. Both Suat and I felt strange when I told him we were moving to Istanbul in two days. Yet, we'd both known it was coming; known it, expected it. We were under the tree in the middle of the meadow. He raised his head. Whether he was looking at the sky or the leaves, I couldn't tell. I stared at the dark patches of grass on the famished soil between my knees. From the old garden in the distance, the sound of a frog reached us at intervals. "Look," he said, "only my window is dark." I looked so he wouldn't think that I thought he was talking nonsense. Every room in their house had a light on; only one window on the third floor was dark. The moon illuminated the glass. "If you could see my room now, how large it is, how small it seems. The moon streams down to the head of my bed. Everything grows, swells, everything disappears in the distance," he said. "I've never seen your room at this time of night," I said. "Really, I've never seen it in the moonlight." "Nor will you ever be able to see it. After tonight, the moon will wane, dissolve. And the next time, you'll be in Istanbul." "There can be another time; I can come to see you on a night when the moon is full and glowing again." He said, "You won't"; his voice was distant, restrained, intimate, weighed down, defeated. I wanted to shout, laugh, tell him he was talking nonsense, he was crazy, I wanted to tell him that he knew I had no other friend in the world, that he was denying me, himself, denying the friendship, by saying, by thinking, such a thing, my mouth was brimming with words I didn't utter, my jaws were clenched, I felt as if I was suffocating. I couldn't even raise my head. Couldn't laugh. "I will come," I said, as if my life depended on it. "No, you won't," he said, "you'll forget me. We're not even childhood friends. We grew up side by side but we are both alone, each separate. We played together. We know each other inside out, perhaps. We've spent each night together for two years . . . Even went out fishing . . . Still . . ."

## I

I slowly walked backward. When my hand touched the doorknob, a sound startled me. Then, a distant, exhausted voice asked, "Who's there?" From behind the door blocked by Suat's childhood bed, the voice asked again, "Who's there?" and dissolved. "It's Mushfik," I said. "Suat, is that you, is that you?" The voice sounded heavy, drawn out, as if it would never be extinguished. A vast silence followed her last word. As though everything, all that once defied silence, fell silent. "It's me Auntie, it's Mushfik," I said. I left Suat's room and entered his mother's room.

## II

"I will come," I said. "Still, you won't come, because you'll forget all this, none of this is important, we've been playing up until now. And games are soon forgotten. What will remain of them?" I felt guilty, I felt guilty on all counts, the more Suat spoke, the more guilt I felt. I wanted to shout, let everyone know about my guilt, I wanted to . . . I thought of some words about love. The soil was parched between my knees. The patches of grass were dry. I think I stretched my legs. "But those days when we told them we were going out fishing—" He cut me off, "Yes, we used to catch a couple of fish, just so we could show that we had and then we played with each other in the dark, I know . . ." "You call that play?" was all I could say. "Of course. It was play, what we did. Neither you nor I could find a person closer to us, so we played with each other. It could have been somebody else, and nothing would have been any different. We played. Because we were able to do nothing but play. Why don't you want to admit it?" He was being cruel. Beginning to be like the other members of the Çuhaci family. I tried not to think about how my mother had endured her anger in silence without revealing it, perhaps because her dignity would not let her say anything to me. I tried not to think about how she gradually grew distant and cold toward me because she knew of my meetings with Suat every night, she knew that I went out fishing with him, and why I really went. Even the ground began growing dark. Then the wind started blowing. The frog made a gurgling sound, as if to say it was about to stop altogether. Much later, Suat said, "Forgive me if I hurt you. I have to go." He didn't have to. Most likely, nobody but his mother was waiting for him, and she must have fallen asleep by now. He had a key. Unlike me. He didn't have to worry about having to go to a hotel, as I had to last week. This time I wouldn't go to the hotel. I'd enter the house through the basement window instead. Nobody was waiting for Suat. All the lights in the windows had been turned off. He had nothing pressing. Still, he wanted to go. "Tomorrow morning," I said, "would you come tomorrow morning? Come to the lighthouse, six o'clock, when it's still cool, we can take the boat. Will you come?" He was standing, the moon at his back. I knew his face by heart. "Yes," he said. I sensed that he was walking away. Beneath me, the soil was turning dark. I realized suddenly how much the hotel clerk's eyes resembled

Suat's. Their clarity. A rooster crowed. My eyes are green too, but not liquid green, not the moist, sunburned green that yearns for the sea. The rest of the roosters began crowing in succession. The green of Suat's eyes was washed out, a different green from that of the hotel clerk's eyes, but I had had to see the clerk's eyes in order to understand Suat's. The roosters continued crowing. Suat's window remained dark as I walked from the meadow to the road, from the road to the back gate of our yard. Perhaps he was asleep, I thought, perhaps he didn't turn on his light because he knew I would be waiting to see it, I told myself. I think I felt ashamed. But I know I feared that he wouldn't be able to wake up and come, that he wouldn't come. I can't remember how I slept that night.

From a distance, he was coming like a song . . .

## I

I could barely see her head among the crumpled sheets. Stretched out, she lay there like a robust flower. The room smelled. The soap smell on the sheets in which she had wrapped herself, a habit from childhood, was mixed with the smell of dust that had set in, which gnawed at the fabric and stayed despite countless cleanings. But there was also a faintly acrid smell that was stronger than the others. A smell that became more familiar, more distinct as I approached the bed: the smell of alcohol. Her body discernible among the folds of the sheets, she straightened her neck, raised her head briefly, and let it fall. "I thought you were Suat," the voice was more animated than before, though still weighed down by an infinite grief. "Why did you come? Why didn't Suat come? Where is my son?" Then suddenly, "Don't you know where he is? Why didn't he come instead of you?" "Dear—" I attempted to say something. Tossing her head violently, she began to shout, "No no no no no no I am not your dear or anything if you loved me at all you would have visited Suat more often and told him not to abandon me like this no no no no no you don't love me neither you nor Suat where is Suat tell me tell me now where is Suat?" Her head stopped moving abruptly. She frowned as if her stomach was churning. I didn't know how to respond. "You leave me alone like this, all alone, and then wonder why I became sick. You don't love me, you don't. You don't love me." Exhausted, she stopped. I came a step closer. Her feeble, bony hand emerged from the folds of the sheets and reached out to me. "Come, come by my side. I have spent all my life alone. Come, stay a little while, don't leave yet, Suat isn't here, come over to me at least, sit by my side." Her voice was fading. I walked through the sweaty smell. Her head sank in the pillow, her waist rose. The sheet began taking on her form. Her hand in the air, she was waiting for me to come near her. When she could grab my arm, she pulled me over. I sat down. "Here, come. You've both grown older, you no longer listen to me. I am sick but still you don't take pity on me." The sun coming through the window hit me first. Aunt Nimet's hands were quivering on my arm in the sunlight. Her words dissolved in the sunlight. She stared at the wall and much later was able to speak again, "Why did you come? Didn't you know Suat wouldn't be here?" Everything was muted by the sun. No sound other than her voice could be heard. "We're leaving tomorrow," I said with difficulty. "I came to say good-bye, dear Auntie, since we're leaving. " "Doesn't Suat know that you're leaving, that you'd come? Then why did he leave the house?" I couldn't answer. "What did you say?" She stared at the sunlight that was hitting my face. "What did you say?" Her muffled voice deepened. "Are you leaving? Are you all leaving?" "Yes, going to Istanbul. For good. That's where we'll be settling. You'll come to see us, won't you? Of course, I'll be coming to visit Sarikum from time to time. I'll come with my mother. Right, Auntie? Isn't that so, Auntie?" I stopped suddenly, exhausted. I didn't know what else to say. My parched throat, my breathlessness scared me. "Father always wanted to open a store there," I tried to say. I couldn't even hear my own words. Her right eye was pinned on mine. Silence. Her parted lips didn't move. A ray of sunlight fell on her left eye. My arm began to grow numb under the icy weight of her hand.

## II

From a distance, he was coming like a song. In the crimson morning, like a song delayed, hesitant, dark, unhurried, sad, a song that overwhelmed, replenished. I ran down to the sea on the wings of a cool breeze. The weeds had begun giving off their smells. I wondered where the perfectly calm sea came up with the little waves that beat against the shore. I gazed at the pebbles on the edge of the water, listened. At first, the sound of being swept away, then a light rustling, then the sound of the waves breaking. The boat was in its usual place. I went and sat down by it. The pebbles felt cold. I took off my shoes, rolled up my trousers. I pushed the pebbles around and scratched at the wet sand with my toes. Suat was coming down the sandy path. Watching from the corner of my eye, I waited for him to reach the pebble shore. I kept my head lowered. His navy blue canvas rubber-soled shoes stopped next to me. Facing the sea, his wrinkled pants covering his thin legs were caught in a breeze. I still didn't raise my head. I reached for his thin, bony ankle, held it, squeezed it. Then I sensed that he wanted to sit down. I squeezed his ankle even more tightly. He stiffened, didn't move, didn't budge. I slowly raised my head. He had been looking at me. I saw his face touched by grief. It was beautiful. He was beautiful. It was as if I were seeing his face for the first time. He was smiling.

It was a brand-new, unfamiliar face that I had never seen before. His eyes, sunken in their hollows, shaded by his eyebrows, green, washed-out, pure green. His slender nose, its angled tip, swollen nostrils. His prominent chin, his large open mouth, leaving exposed his milk-white teeth. Locks of his hair fell over his eyebrows. He was beautiful in the faint delicate light. Once again, the thought of sin entered my mind. I was happy that, until that moment, I had seldom looked him in the face, that I had always kept my eyes on some other place when talking to him. I was discovering his familiar face all over again. I was drawn to it. It was beautiful. Then I pulled at his ankle, as if to say I wanted him to sit down. He did, slowly. I let go of his ankle. We hadn't spoken yet. The shimmering sea opened, stretched restlessly before us. At the base of the lighthouse, the rocks broke through the waves sharply; the gentle waves grew louder. "So you woke up early," I said. I understood by his mumbling that he didn't want to talk. I felt like shouting. Then we laid down. "Last night," I said, "what you said . . ." There is a giant rock by the lighthouse, its base is hollow, the top stretches out to the sea, I crept underneath it. He joined me. Our heads were under the rock awning. I said, "What you said were foolish words, you know." "Yes, yes, what matters is to understand each other, we understand each other," he said as if he didn't want to argue, as if to silence me. I remained quiet. I didn't understand. We were silent. The sun began to reflect off the sea. My feet were getting hot. I relaxed, sensed that he was relaxing. I turned my eyes toward his face. He stared back with a sad look in his washed-out green eyes. "Let's go," I said, "weren't we supposed to get in the boat?"

The sun hit my eyes. I still looked in his direction. My fingers trailed along his lips, his eyes, got caught in his hair. I pulled my hand away. "Get up, let's go." Mumbling, he brushed my hand away; I let go of his fingers. I went over to the boat, tossed my shoes inside, "Get up," I said again. At long last, we sailed off.

# I

At first, her knees began to shake. I could feel their hollow beating against my waist. Then her lips closed, her hands came to life, her eyes reopened; with a deep sigh, she said, "Don't go, don't leave yet." I could barely understand. The sun was no longer shining on my head. Suat wasn't coming, wouldn't be coming. Last night, I hoped childishly that he would appear under the tree. He wouldn't. But the rest of the Çuhaci family would soon return to fill up their house. In the distance, I thought I heard children's voices coming from the road. With an effort, I tried again. Suddenly her eyes opened wide, her thin cheeks began to shake. Her hands stiffened, like iron. "You won't leave, you'll stay, you two can't leave me alone like this. I don't care if your mother and father leave. How many times have they come to see me, when have they been friends to me? But you can't leave. I can't be left alone alone alone." Her voice was growing sharper. "When Suat is not around, you are like a son. You are my son, my other son." The smell of alcohol had grown stronger. "Suat gets angry when I drink. As if he has any right to be angry. On account of him, I endured the clan, the whole lot of them, both before his father died and afterward. In this room, an outcast in their midst, I felt alien, isolated, endured their animosity, their strangeness, silenced my own heart. Do you understand? On account of him, all for him. I didn't say anything when he began leaving at nights, coming back in the mornings. Yet I knew he loved me, I thought he did. I see the others only in the evenings anyway. The food they put in my mouth sticks in my throat but still I don't leave the house. Just so his life is not interrupted. They see him and I can't. Do you understand? How can you? You're his friend. You're like him, too." Her head sank onto the pillow with a dry thud. "Get up, go get me the medicine bottle." She was facing the wall. "Hurry up, give me that bottle." I saw that she had let go of my arm, though

I hadn't felt it. "What are you waiting for? It's in the top drawer of the dresser. Hurry." There was a bottle of pills in the drawer. "You still can't find it?" The wall muffled her voice. "A tall bottle." Under the handkerchiefs, the scarves, I noticed the tip of a brown bottle, took it out, and gave it to her. She pulled the cork and pressed the bottle to her lips. The sharp smell brought me to my senses. She had already pushed the cork back in and shoved the bottle underneath her pillow. "What are you doing, Auntie!" my drowned voice came out sharply. "Mind your own business, don't meddle. You can't understand. You can't understand what loneliness is. Come here beside me." Her face was still turned toward the wall. But her voice was calm. A calm fluid voice weighed down by an immense grief. "Come." She grabbed my arm again, pulled me against her. "Night after night, I waited for him, do you understand? Night after night. I bit my fingertips because I was jealous that he loved you, that he was out with you. Night after night, I waited for him to call for me, to ask me to come to him, even while he was sleeping. When he had a headache, or a cold, on the days when he got sick, I stood watch, my ear at his door, waiting for him to call me the way he used to as a child. There were times I wished he were sick so he would need me. He pulled his bed over and blocked the door. So I wouldn't enter his room. I would have jumped over it. If he had just called. But he never did. Alone at night, I waited in vain. With each passing night, my solitude grew worse. Then I started drinking." Self-pity. She was pleading now. Her hand still clenched my arm. "I felt free when the clan left the house. Like today. They went to Demirli. All of them. They are supposed to return very late. I've been alone in the house since morning. Haven't even eaten. Alone, by myself . . ." Her voice became a murmur. "So I've been drinking since morning. So what if Suat sees me in this state when he returns? . . ." "He'll be sad. Do you want him to be sad, Auntie?" "So what if he's sad? I've had my share of sadness on account of him. Besides, what do you care?" I had to leave. "Anyway, he wouldn't be sad, wouldn't be. When he returns late at night, he doesn't stop by my room. The next morning he says he didn't want to wake me up. He wouldn't even come to see me . . ." I had to leave. The calm in her voice encouraged me. Suddenly, the loud buzz of a fly on the glass filled the house. I attempted to leave. "I should be going, Auntie." Her hand slid off my arm, fell among the folds of the sheets. Suddenly her body turned rigid. She began tossing her head hopelessly against the pillow again. She stared at me wide-eyed, as if she no longer saw me. She began dejectedly, "No no no no no don't leave don't leave yet no no . . ." The faster she threw her head back and forth, the more her body stiffened. Her torso arched like a bridge between her head and legs. "Mushfik dear Mushfik don't leave don't leave yet stay by me don't leave me alone . . ." Her eyes grew heavy. "I beg you stay don't leave what would I do without you wait a while still Mushfik dear dear Mushfik . . ." Her hands kept rising in the air and falling like claws. "I have to go Auntie, I have to. I must leave but I will write you letters. I will come back. I will come back for you. We'll see each other often." The words rushed madly out of my mouth. "I must leave now. I still have a lot to do. We're leaving tomorrow morning, imagine . . ." I stretched out my hand, she pulled at it. "Come here, at least let me give you a kiss since you won't come back will you come back . . ." She was pulling, with all her might, she was pulling at me. "I'll come during the holiday, I will, I promise, Auntie." "Holiday what holiday still a long time before the holiday you're lying aren't you how long until the holiday?" The sharp smell of alcohol struck my face. "A month and a half." "A month and a half?" Her entire weight, her entire strength centered in her hand. "No you wouldn't you wouldn't come are you telling the truth will you come in a month and a half?" "Of course I will. I will definitely come. Straight here." "What am I to do for a month and a half all alone? Suat will leave me again though perhaps he won't since you'll no longer be around . . ." Her body was still arched, her head still tossing from side to side. As for her voice, it had grown fuller, less desperate. "Come dear Mushfik come stay a bit let me kiss you before you leave . . ." Her movements became slower, calm. I leaned toward her. In the vast silence, the fly on the glass ruled over all. She closed her eyes. She clasped my temples. Her mouth, heavy with the smell of alcohol, passed from cheek to cheek and across my mouth, and drew a moist line along my face. Suddenly, she let go of me; I withdrew. "Leave now, go, we'll be glad to see you back some day. Go, son, farewell, give my regards to your mother. Have a safe trip. Farewell, my child, farewell." Her voice was quiet, distant, as if coming from the abyss of shame. Walking backward, I left the room. I didn't even go by Suat's room. The stairwell felt dark, warm, fluid. Waves of darkness streamed toward the coolness downstairs. As if diving into the sea, I tore through the clammy heat. I don't think the steps creaked. Right outside the door, I was greeted by a breeze, and felt the stale heat closing in behind me. My sweat was drying. The rest of the Çuhaci family had gone to Demirli. They would return late at night. I was in no hurry to face the scalding sun. I stood in the breeze, perhaps expecting Suat to appear.

## II

I was rowing toward Demirli. He was napping in the front of the boat, still in a bad mood, his hand dangling in the water. Much later, we stopped across the sandbank between Demirli and the light-house. The oars felt lighter. At first I heard a light gurgling, then the sand under the boat gave a rasping sound. I jumped into the water. We had crossed over the seaweed. I nudged Suat. He came to life. Rolling up his sleeves, he jumped in. We anchored the boat and let it float loose. It drifted a little distance and began to bob idly. The sun had waxed considerably. The sand was beginning to sizzle. By now in Sarikum, between the lighthouse and the fisherman Arif's house, lots of people would be going in the water. No one lived behind the lighthouse since the doll maker Osman had died. We were all alone between Demirli and the lighthouse. In the distance, the yellow meadow was bordered by the tiny houses of Sarikum on the one end, and those of Demirli on the other. I wanted to shout, but whispered in his ear instead, "What did you mean when you said 'understanding'?" "We understand each other, that's all." He fell silent again. Past the shore where the meadow began, we lay in the shadow of a great fig tree. The grass was scorching us all over again. The sea was immersed in the sunlight and made us drowsy as it always had. We were sweating in the shade. The sharp smell of warm sweat filled the space between us. The shade was like the bottom of a well, its cool gradually dissolving as the sun baked its periphery. I was still trying to speak. Then one of Suat's fingers touched mine. The shade cooled us briefly only to dissolve again. I was fighting silence, trying to speak. When my third finger also got caught in his fingers, I responded. Then all our fingers clenched together, his hand filling mine. Immersed in a sea of heat, I began learning about the softness of his hand, coming to know it. The sea billowing, his hand braided in mine. I pulled our hands toward me and rested them on my belly. Our shoulders were touching. Then our hands gave in to their habitual madness. Suddenly I opened my eyes. His were closed. He wasn't moving. He was sweating, so was I. We were now inside an enormous sun. Dissolving. The fervent sea reverberated around us.

The sun crossed over the hill. The heat was growing intense, swallowing the shade, pushing it toward our feet. We relaxed. I leaned back. It felt as though days had passed by. His head grew heavy on my shoulder. A train whistle reached us from a distance. I saw its smoke on the edge of the meadow. He lay there without opening his eyes or stretching his legs. My arm grew numb under his head. Suat looked like a jagged line on the dry soil. Suddenly I felt hungry. I looked around, although I knew there was nothing to curb my hunger beside sleep. Right then, a pair of eyes caught mine. Staring straight at me, green eyes crossed by a thin black stripe. Jet-black. Slender, agile. I couldn't figure out when it came or from where. I stretched out my hand; its startled muscles sent shivers through the jet-black coat. "Pusu," I called, it raised its ears. "Come," I said, trying to stretch my hand out further. It leapt back, flashed into the open field, and disappeared. Then another train passed. The sea was awakening. I nudged Suat. "I want to sleep," he said. As we walked toward the water he kept his eyes closed. I pulled the boat toward us, we got in. I lifted up the anchor, and sat at the oars. Against the sun, his beautiful face looked sorrowful. I sailed off. In the depths, he opened his eyes. Green, washed-out, clear, luminous. His prominent chin moved, his large mouth opened, exposing his milk-white teeth, he yawned, locks of his hair fell over his eyebrows. There was a breeze. He began to undress.

In the sea's invigorating coolness, we began a chase, swimming around the boat, trying to catch each other; whenever we held onto the boat, we would look at our green flesh and laugh.

He took the oars as I put on my clothes. He wanted to show that he was stronger than I was. It was hot again. The sweat drying on my shirt now gave off a sharp smell. I snatched the oars from his hands. I felt a hardening inside. Suat couldn't have been more beautiful, in fact, he shouldn't be. When he laughed, his lips would curl, relax. When we brought the boat to the shore at the usual spot, we were both silent. We climbed the sandy path and, crossing the road, began walking alongside the wheat fields. The hardening I felt inside remained blind to the green, the beauty, the drowned beauty of the drowned green. "Mushfik," he said. I looked inside those green eyes. "You'll come next month, won't you?" I closed my eyes, nodded as if to say, "Yes." He fell silent. He took my arm. I thought I could bear his weight on my arm for the rest of my life. I felt the hardness recede somewhat. When we reached the tracks, he pulled his hand away. Suddenly, the hardness returned. We shook hands. "It's best if I leave you here. At home, they'll be wondering . . ." "Kiss your mother's hand for me. Tomorrow I want to stop by and say good-bye," I said. He looked happy. The sun was hitting the roof of their house. He walked away in the light, dissolved. The hardness remained. We would be leaving in one day. I began to realize that one couldn't avoid dying. Yet, something significant and unforgettable would always remain. There was no yesterday, I wouldn't know tomorrow, even today did not exist. Only hardness did. "Death," I said, "death . . ."

# I

Outside, I was greeted by silence broken by the sounds of chickens and cats. At night, I waited for him in the house. I hadn't wanted to go and wait beneath the tree. I'm sure he didn't go there either.

This morning, as always, the train crossed the vast meadow between Sarikum and Demirli. In the distance, the fig tree looked like a stain on the sea. We would not return to Sarikum tonight, tomorrow morning, the day after tomorrow, or the night after tomorrow. I knew. He knew.

1954–1955

# AND HOW COME I REMEMBER NOW . . .

One day he said something, I recall, something about women, no, no, you women he said, and I was offended, angry, don't be angry he said, obviously you want to yell again, but hush and listen, I am sick and tired of all this yelling he said, and I don't know why I agreed to remain quiet then, I shouldn't have when he said you women, but I did something stupid, just as I have all my life, had I not been this stupid I would not have let his father in, may God bless his soul, may he rest in peace, the poor man, the only one who truly loved me, and I didn't marry him, couldn't marry him, that cursed accident took him from me, had I not been stupid neither would I have married Reshit, that is, if the thing, if he had not happened, who knows, I could have been better off, no, perhaps worse off, still, all on account of him, all because I loved him, because I was madly attached to him even before he was born, from the first time I felt him inside, kicking, for him I accepted the pastry man's hand and he shuts me off, attempts to silence me, even though it was impossible for him not to love me, even though I knew it was impossible for him not to love me, even though he knew he could find no other woman, or even another man, ever to love him more than I do, he gave me grief, shut me off, how I agreed to remain silent that day, how I didn't kick him out of the room, how I didn't cast myself in the sea, and he says you women, you women, as if I were just any woman, you women, when you get attached to something you get blind and don't see any flaw even if it hits you in the eye, you don't see, he says, I am not saying you can't see, I am not saying you pretend not to see, I am saying you don't see, you don't because you're blind, he says, supposedly I didn't see his flaws, as if I didn't see his flaws, as if I didn't silence my heart and take in each day like poison and spend sleepless nights, and I'd still remain quiet, say nothing, was it because I didn't see his flaws, of course I pretended not to see, and he knew it too, and still he dares to say, I am not saying you pretend not to see, I am saying you don't see, because if you had the eye to see you wouldn't be a woman he says, for him to call me woman, to call his mother woman, after I carried him in my womb and endured everything just for him, of course I am a woman, I am but I shouldn't be in his eyes, besides, what's left of the woman ever since he took shape in my womb, you don't see because you're blind, he says, yes, those days are gone, gone and over with, far away from me, distances came between us, between our bodies, our rooms, our meals, between our warmth, even though he has no one else besides me and I have no one else besides him, even though we seemingly lived slept woke up in the same house, he distanced himself from me and then one day, out of nowhere he returned, our paths crossed again, you know how they tell of rats abandoning a sinking ship, just like that, everybody apparently abandoned him, and when he was left all alone I came to his mind, perhaps he realized he was falling ill, my baby returned to me, my goodness, I had not thought of this until now, I thought he became ill when he returned and saw me, I thought he couldn't bear the fact that he had to come back to me, I thought he couldn't stand me, it never occurred to me, forgive me God, forgive me for wronging my son, I don't know perhaps I am mistaken but, no, I am certain, certain that he knew he was falling ill, he sensed he was falling ill and returned to me, and I tried to show him I was hurt, it's my fault, my sin, dear God forgive me, I totally forgot him, was seized by my womanness, my eyes grew blind, I didn't see what I should have seen, what I should have been able to see, he was right perhaps, he, too, was right but,

forgive me dear God, I still can't get it out of my mind that he fell ill as soon as he returned to me, I say illness even when talking to myself, I don't want to let any word but illness cross my mind and what he had was an illness, his mind got all scrambled, he went mad, he was afraid to go out on the street, they'll kill me, he was saying, don't you hear the voices, the uproar, he was saying, there is a war going on outside God is punishing the world he has released the devil to punish the world all men will die I don't want to die only the pregnant women will survive and bear children but not all are good women not all are good but the children ought to be good and they will defeat the devil and recover the path to God become men loved by God the women won't die, my God, how his words still ring in my ears, as if he were saying them by my ear just now, then the guns and cannons slowly hushed, and he calmed down, no longer anxious, dear God, he was saying, no one besides the children can find you any more, no one besides the children whose eyes are not sullied by the foul earth can reach you, by then he was walking around the house, we didn't keep him in bed, but whenever someone came by, as soon as he heard the doorbell ring, he'd run to his room, lock his door, and stay inside, in those times I'd be seized by fear, though I knew he wouldn't answer if I knocked on his door, so I'd peek through the keyhole, see him crouched in one corner, sitting on the floor, I'd given up hope for his recovery, forgive me dear God, I had given up on you as well, forgive me, forgive me, later he kept rambling about glasses, wherever he saw glasses he would break them, saying that the blind had no use for glasses, then one day he asked for his own glasses, you broke them I told him but he couldn't remember, how did I break them, mama, he asked, I realized then that he'd recovered from his illness, I thanked You, dear God, again You had taken me by my hand and lifted me, I prostrated myself, dear God, forgive me,

when I saw he no longer hated me, I didn't know what to do out of joy, so I was blind, I was truly blind not to see that he didn't hate me, it was illness that had overtaken him, that's why he had acted so, he had started quarreling as soon as he had returned to me, he would call me mother and then fight me, then he got ill, then recovered, but he left me again, five streets came between us, this time five streets and thirty-nine doors, he comes by and I also go to him but he doesn't want to move back home, when he visits he doesn't even go near his room, as though his madness is locked in the room and waiting for him, he is afraid of the room, of its door even, but what matters is he is calm now, he stays in his place, writes and reads, works too, comes by every month, saying, dear mother, here is your money, and leaves me something, I am happy, happy that he is well, he leaves the money, doesn't stay long, asks me when I'd visit him, I tell him when and his face lights up, though I don't want to trouble him with frequent visits, and he still calls me when I delay going, dear God, why couldn't he move back in, he'd even have a different room, the house is mine after all, it's Reshit's greatest gift to me, it provides me with enough income to go on living, may God bless his soul, Reshit was very good to me, true, I am speaking ill of him, though much of my life's burden is also on account of him, in any case, it's not time to talk about Reshit,

he doesn't want to come back now, but I wait, hope that he'll come one day, he'll grow tired, exhausted, of everything and then return to me, full of dejection but no longer ill, my God will forgive and send him back to me, full of dejection he'll arrive and my arms will still be open, he knows how I wait for him, he knows he knows he knows,

how come I remember now that day, I still can't forget his words, and I just remember on whose account we got to fighting, on account of his friend, he used to prefer his worthless friend over me, perhaps he still does but he no longer comes to talk to me about those he loves, probably he thinks I am not jealous anymore, he no longer taunts me with every one of his affairs, he used to, now he thinks I've given up being jealous, whereas I still am, I still am jealous, how can I not be jealous of all his friends and lovers, all those with whom I must share his love, but when have I made it known to him, whatever I told him I told out of concern for him, how could I agree to his falling in love with just any man, when I was able to like at the most one or two among them, besides, didn't all abandon him, did any one of them visit when he was ill, besides, none ever loved him, he loved, burned, lost sleep, tried all he could for them, ruined his days and nights in their name, having them around was enough for him, he never wanted to be loved, didn't I know this also, but now he no longer tells me anything, peace, he says now and then, peace, he says and smiles, if he could also learn being loved,

back then he used to tell me, you're jealous, shame on you, he'd tell me, when I wouldn't admit even to myself that I was jealous, how he dared to utter those words, saying, all you women, so this was our flaw, true, we wouldn't want our loved one to be flawed, and if he were, we would overlook his flaw, but, no, he said, we were blind and that's why we wouldn't see, I disagreed that day, I told him that one woman can see truths better than ten men can, he refused to believe, he didn't understand, besides, he never listened to me back then, then again, when did he ever want to, he used to do all the talking, and if I ever attempted to say something, he'd quickly want to cut me off, of course, I wouldn't mince my words, when I'd tell him you're angry because I am telling the truth, he'd blow his top, spew every which word that reached his mouth and poison the day for both of us, besides, when did I ever tell him something false, when did I ever say anything uncalled for, but obviously he couldn't stand hearing the truth, they all wanted me to tell lies, all my life, first his father and I lived a life of lies, and how hard I tried to keep him from discovering, from hearing about the lies, if it were up to me, I wouldn't even want him to talk to others, but Reshit, and the poor man really tried to be a father to him, and how he loved him, and Mushfik, too, almost respected him, though not once did he give him a hug, smile at him or call him father, not even to please him, as though he knew, but he couldn't have known, how could he have known, later when he was ill, he kept saying things but I didn't dwell on them, goodness, I hadn't thought of them till just now, I also must have forgotten what he said, but he couldn't have known, well, he was a suspicious child, his father, his father was an exceptional man, he loved me a great deal, neither he nor Reshit ever found fault in anything I said, yes, there were days when we were cross with each other and Reshit always knew that I preferred remaining silent rather than saying something wrong, and when I did talk he'd understand it was true and tell me that I knew best, but Mushfik, my very own son, he never wished to tell me anything like that, if you asked him, everything I said was wrong, everything crooked, but never mind, the dear Lord must have wanted to test me that day and made my son say all those things,

why am I obsessing over this, anyway, I don't know, it just occurred to me, all you women are blind when you love a man, you don't see even the slightest of his flaws, no, he didn't say, the slightest flaw, he said something else, you don't see any of his flaws but let him commit the slightest indiscretion against you, yes, that's what he said, then another sort of curtain falls over your eyes and he is the worst man in the world, even if he tried and caught a bird with his mouth just to please you, and that's no lie, I agree, if someone is good he is good, bad if he is bad, can any good come from someone who breaks your heart, now he broke my heart plenty of times but he is my son, I tolerate him no matter what, forgive him, love him as always, of course, it'd be better if he didn't break my heart, but which son doesn't, and if the mother loves her son as much as I do, though could you even find mothers who love their sons as much as I do, who among them sacrificed herself as much as I have, who among them gave up her youth on account of her son, ah, how come these thoughts rush into my mind, my sleep lost, where do they come from, now, in the middle of the night, does he know that I still lose sleep, toss and turn in bed for him, even if he knows, does he understand, perhaps he gets angry, but, no, he doesn't, he no longer would, perhaps he has learned to be loved, perhaps he has learned the peace of being loved, just the other day, we were both lost in thought, and suddenly, mother, he said, love is the only path to God, both of us have sought it all our lives, you couldn't find it but I did, the right way to eat, drink, dress, sleep, to love a singular person, to offer one's heart's burden to God as a debt of gratitude, all this you have sought and I found at last, he said, can anyone say such things unless he has learned being loved,

but even if now he knows how to be loved, he still wouldn't under-stand, still wouldn't want me to lose sleep over him, my blessed mother, may she rest in peace, why did she visit me in my dream, is something going to happen again, there I was, our house had plenty of windows overlooking the sea but I loved one in partic-ular, when sitting on the sofa, I'd see the entire coast, all the way from Hisar to Arnavutköy, I had Mushfik in my lap, I was breast-feeding him, he was making those gurgling sounds while enjoying my milk and even though I was afraid he'd choke himself I couldn't pull my breast from his mouth, his eyes would slide, squint, and close from pleasure each time he swallowed, I couldn't look at him enough, I was crying, thinking about his father who didn't get to see his baby, Reshit must not have been around yet, I must not have been married to him yet, I was all alone in the room, ships were passing in the distance, though few used to pass in front of our mansion, suddenly a ship appeared at the pier, blew its horn, it was death, the ship, it had come to take my baby away, Mushfik still wouldn't let go of my breast, I was holding him tightly, the ship blew its horn again, it was a piercing, rending sort of sound, I must have been all alone in the house, after the ship blew its horn one more time, it suddenly began moving, when I looked out the other window, I couldn't see it any more, then the door to the room opened, my mother entered, I was startled, I kept pressing Mushfik against my breast, my mother, mother dearest came near me, with her pure white face, her delicate snow-white hair and pitch-black dress, don't be scared my child, she said, no one can take your baby away from you, what woman has ever lost her son to others, I've never heard such a thing, a woman would rather die than give up her child, then she looked at his face, this child is full, don't you see, she said, why are you still feeding him, he's sleepy and about to fall asleep, give him to me, I looked at my mother's face, the woman in front of me wasn't my sweet-faced mother, she was a conniving stranger with an evil face who wanted to take my child away, Mushfik's eyes were closed but from pleasure, he wasn't full yet, he was still sucking, I could still feel the milk oozing from my bones and pouring into my breast, how could I let him go, I told her, didn't you just say that a woman would rather die than give up her child, that she'd protect him even if she had to die, then she laughed, then I suddenly found myself in the middle of the meadow, she was laughing, chasing me, Mushfik was still in my arms sucking my breast, there was no more milk, my son started crying, I was running, chased by the woman, her laughter mixed with my son's cries, then I saw my mother in the distance, her arms were open, she was calling me, hurry, come, she is exhausted, can't catch up with you, I was climbing the hill, panting, the woman remained far below, I was almost in my mother's arms, Mushfik was crying incessantly, mother, I said, my milk dried up, she nodded, just when I reached her, she suddenly disappeared, vanished, Mushfik stopped crying, bit my breast, then turned his face, I woke up, drenched in sweat, lost my sleep, when Mushfik had turned his face toward me, his eyes seemed to say, you are a bad mother, your milk dried up, how can a mother's milk dry up from fear, what was my fault, when did I ever turn him down, was I at fault whenever I warned him against mixing with those boys, did I ever open my mouth and say a word whenever he brought them home, even though they were rude and bad, yes he loved the boys but I always could see their flaw, is that why women are wrong, is it because they speak the truth, ah, I wish I could sleep a little, I should go and see him tomorrow, I should kiss and caress his hair and overlook all his flaws, forgive him, dear God, forgive me, if I am a woman, am I not still a mother?

long ago, just to please him, I used to tell tales to him and his friends, once I was cross with him, he was four at the time, I was leaving him at home and going out, he was watching me go, I saw him from the corner of my eye, his face full of wrinkles as if he was about to cry, suddenly a terrible aura of hopelessness came upon him, if you leave me, he said, I will call the Arab and ask him to devour me, what would it take, what would it take for him to say the same thing now, to ask me, mother, how about a fairy tale, what would it take?

1954–1956

# THE KEY

Through the glass, I watched the cats bathing in sunlight. Alaja, the calico, was sprawled out as though her belly was full; she kept blinking her eyes, watching me, her mouth agape, her teeth old, overgrown. Farther down, the black-and-white Bebek stood poised, tense with wakeful muscles—his big claws rolled into balls. His eyes were wide open, their large green slits staring straight at me. He stood frozen on the scorching stones. The kitten—as yet unnamed, slight, shaky, less than two months old and unaware of his youth—walked back and forth between his mother and brother. First he would attack his mother's tail, then, getting no response from her, he would sprawl his body before his brother. A pure white patch ran from his belly to his chin, stopped at the pink of his lips, tongue, and gums. Bebek remained unmoved, resisting the fawning and teasing around him. Then, suddenly, he sprang into motion. His tail pulsing with anger, he grabbed the kitten and started biting. The calico stayed put; the kitten struggled, caught in his brother's fangs and claws, crying bitterly. I tapped on the glass. Bebek raised his ears and turned to stare at me with his sinister green eyes; he froze again. The kitten shook himself free, then threw himself again at Bebek's paws.

Hans (his mother could never leave the side of the big, furry, slumbering Viennese Persian that lived with the Germans who came to Sarikum for the summers; therefore, I didn't much object to giving him a German name; besides, we tried calling him Firuz for a while but he didn't like it, so we settled on Hans) used to stare at me from the very depths of male solitude. He would stand in front of me and fix his yellow eyes on mine. Perfectly silent, staring. He had arrived at our house shortly after our dog had died. The first thing he did was walk to all the corners where the dog smell had set in and sniff them one by one, then he sat forlorn in the middle of the kitchen and stared at me. From that first day on, he did not meow in the house. When I read a book or opened my eyes in the morning, he would materialize beside me, try to speak, eager to receive my attention. I would keep my head on the pillow and close my eyes again. Then he would approach, stand between the book and my eyes, lean sideways against my pillow and string together all the sounds he could muster; still, I would not look. "What do you want?" I would ask; the slight, muffled, tiny mutterings coming from his throat never sounded catlike. As if he were trying to speak, to tell me something. After a while, I would look into his eyes, then he would calm down and begin to purr.

In the crowded, concrete solitude of Istanbul, he had grown mute. Within a month or two, he quit speaking altogether.

Only his spryness, his supple mass remained unchanged. Then one day, he went down to the street and was run over by a car. I took him in my arms and carried him to the garden—composed of a few sickly trees and the poor soil under them that had somehow withstood the onslaught of concrete, smog, and charcoal dust; his body was still warm, his tail and hind legs caught under the wheels were stone-stiff but his neck seemed alive, his eyes were open, his honey-frost coat was lined with thin trails of blood. Hans, I called, but he didn't speak, didn't look. I found the softest spot under the trees and dug his hole—the same spot where Reshit Bey always asked to have his table set as soon as the sunny days arrived so he could resume his custom of drinking under a breezy tree, from the first warm day until the end of autumn, as he used to do in Sarikum.

That evening, Reshit Bey (should I call him father, since back then I hadn't yet learned that he wasn't my father and knew him as father) heard about Hans's death while his table was being set. "That ought to teach you a lesson," he said to me. "I told you Istanbul is not Sarikum, told you not to bring the poor animal along, you remember, don't you, I told you so while you were trying to cram the animal into the basket, told you the city wasn't for him, something would happen to him, I told you all this, didn't I?" I had told him nothing about Hans lying under the patch of soil where he had his table set; let him drink over his dead body, I thought to myself.

He asked me to bring him more cigarettes when the pack in front of him was finished. Mother and I—still true to the Sarikum custom—were sitting behind the screened window in the kitchen. Mother was trying to conceal her happiness at having returned to Istanbul after so many years. There were no stars any more, nor Derecik, nor the war years, nor her aunt; everything had disappeared, even the Second World War had passed; she was tired, and at that moment, when she sensed the beginning of an unraveling beyond her childhood fancy—even my childhood fancy—she was thinking of nothing but savoring the happiness of being back in Istanbul, the happiness that she had tried concealing even from me; I would always come after finishing my homework and sit beside her to watch my father—Reshit Bey—drink, like in the old days, and to remember the last evenings in Sarikum, a year ago. Suat would enter my thoughts, the sea, the stars I could no longer see, the evenings we had returned without fish, the evenings without even a hotel room, without cats, the solitary fig tree on the way to

Demirli, Suat, my loneliness, my hunger, everything would come back to me, my fists would tighten, my arms would tense, my teeth would clench.

I knew that I and no one else could overcome my loneliness, but how? I didn't know. Stiff, frozen, I would remain seated in front of the window and watch my father—Reshit Bey—drink. He seemed free of worries. As if he had found at last what he had been looking for. In Sarikum, he had harvested his crop of hopes, though, by distancing himself from us altogether. How he had done it, we didn't know. Neither Mother nor I did.

I would watch him, but also see behind him Hasene Hanim's wooden fence, wooden house, the concrete wall where our old well used to be. Above his head stretched the lines—hanging on them, clothes that belonged to the upstairs neighbors whom I didn't know, whom I didn't care to know, clothes that were hung clean in the morning and speckled with charcoal dust by the time they were collected in the evening, clothes that I found strange.

Reshit Bey was drinking in the dark again; again he didn't want the kitchen light turned on, but he was still visible in the light coming from the upstairs windows—the pale light absorbed by the concrete wall. Suddenly, he searched himself, grabbed the box in front of him, and tore it. I heard him grumble. Mother looked at me, didn't say anything, then turned away. I didn't move. He downed his glass in one gulp, searched the pockets of his trousers. I wondered why it was taking him so long to yell, "Bring me my cigarettes." He stomped his foot on the ground. Where Hans was buried. He attempted to get up, but sat back down again. His voice came, soft, drunk, "Mushfik, sonny, I have cigarettes in my coat pocket, can you bring them to me?" I can, I didn't say. Shuffling in my slippers, I went to their room.

In the blinding, sickly yellow light, I stood motionless, holding in my hand a pack of Yenije and a brass key. A key I knew. It didn't belong to any of our doors. Yet, I had seen it just a few days ago, somewhere else . . .

Father—Reshit Bey—was shouting, "Didn't you find them?" in his drunken voice. I remained quiet. He was waiting for his cigarettes. I was familiar with his impatience. My voice was frozen, I couldn't breathe. A brass key . . . By now, my father's—Reshit Bey's—eyes must have lost interest in the stars' consolation; he must have started casting malicious glances at the screened window behind which he knew my mother was sitting. Then her gentle voice said, Son, did you not find them yet? From the way she said the word, "son," I knew she sensed a threat—no one sensed a threat better than she—you got it right again, I said to myself. (Am I not the same, don't I always know when something is about to happen, don't I know even today that a momentous disruption awaits me?) I could hear my mother's voice. Biting my lips, I held the key in my hand. The coat was hanging there. The pocket had stayed open in the shape of my hand; I hadn't even buttoned it up. Then I dropped the yellow, evil object back into the darkness of the pocket, without knowing, without figuring out to what door it belonged, at the same time sensing that father—Reshit Bey—mustn't know that I had touched the key, that I had seen it.

Now I only held the pack of cigarettes in my hand. Like an unfamiliar thing, or like a stone among the stones I might have collected on a roadside. The comparison made sense. I no longer even knew what I was holding or why I was carrying it. Suddenly I heard the rustling of my mother's skirt next to me. I raised my head and looked. She was staring at me angrily. You know how he gets impatient, you know his mean temper, what's keeping you here so long? Or did you try to smoke? She looked straight into my eyes, waited to see if she was right or not. She knew I had been smoking for some time. It's nothing, Mother, I said, nothing, but I, but I want to tell you something, but wait, let me bring him his cigarettes and then, then, after he goes to bed, I want to tell you something, I think it's something bad, mother, I think, something very bad. Father—Reshit Bey—roared, asking, Are you still looking for the cigarettes? Then his voice quickly died down. Or are you trying to smoke the whole pack? he added quietly. (He must have realized he was no longer in Sarikum.) My mother squeezed my arm. Don't listen to him, she said, I am ashamed of having asked you myself, forgive me, son, go, hurry, be careful. (I knew what being careful meant: not making him angry; not giving him the chance to blow up; letting him be; not forgetting that he was the world's best man when he was sober, that he was drunk, that he was my father even if he hurt me; never opening my mouth to say anything bad or to defy him.) My mind still wrapped up in the evil of the yellow key I couldn't identify, I walked toward the garden, toward the concrete, toward suffocation, toward my father—Reshit Bey—toward the soil under which Hans was buried. The garden had a burned smell tonight; he was taking sips of his drink in the burned smell. As soon as he saw me, he began to yell, but with a muffled, stuttering voice. Where have you been, did you smoke the whole pack, are there any left, one or two maybe? He quieted down, pleased with the pack I handed him. His hands were trembling in the dark, I could tell, the match flame shook, too, his voice had died down, I could only hear his deep breathing. He inhaled, sucking on the cigarette that illuminated his face.

There was a burned smell in the air. I recalled from years ago the memory of Meryem's scorched body, her garden, and I raised my head in terror. But now light was coming only from the flat right above us. There was neither smoke nor flame in the air. But the burned smell still reached my nose. Then I realized it wasn't a burned smell, but the smell of hair, oily, newly dyed, a woman's hair. The smell of a woman's hair, slightly singed, a woman's hair that smelled of an oily dye. Then I saw the dye oozing down her forehead . . .

Why are you standing there, said Father—Reshit Bey—why are you standing? As if you've never seen the sky or me, never seen a man drinking, a man drinking in the dark. As if you've never witnessed the impatience of a man who has been waiting for his cigarettes that he asked his son to fetch hours ago.

I was seeing the dye oozing down her forehead, along the temples, behind the ears toward the neck, oozing. A bright reddish-brown dye on hair we'd known as black. Below the hair, a face, a face covered by oily skin, oily skin whose pores, every one of them, looked like pinholes in a soft fabric. The nose extended down, the face grew thin toward the chin, the eyebrows descended toward the outer corners of the eyes; the face looked as if it was in perpetual sorrow, as if in pain; it looked the way it always did when correcting me . . .

Don't just stand there, repeated my father—Reshit Bey—don't stand there, go back to your mother, go stand where you two spy on me every night, stop looking at the sky, you can look for lost stars some other time, after I'm dead, don't stand in front of me like that.

I ran. The face, mounted on a fat body, came toward me in the dark. Staring, just as it did when it corrected me, its eyes squinting, staring, as if asking, do you like what you did? . . .

As I ran past her, mother grabbed my arm, pulled me to her side. Come, it's not time to run away now, spill the beans, tell me what happened, something must have happened, or you wouldn't have said all you did. I remained silent. She tried again: I saw you, you didn't say a single word to your father, didn't talk back, that's good but not like you, you either didn't hear a word he said or you didn't care, which means your mind was elsewhere. Which is it, tell me, talk to me, son, which is it?

We were resuming our old ways. My fingers pressed into her shoulders, I smelled her hair, mother, mommy, I said. At first she didn't make a sound, a little later, she said, enough son, you're hurting me, but I didn't say a word, enough, tell me what it is, what happened? What suddenly came to your mind? I was pleased to hear her openly admit that she was hurt. Just as I wanted. She had to be hurt, like all women, even when being loved.

Something, mother, something, I began to speak, but I couldn't say it, I wasn't sure yet. Mother, I tried again, inside my father's pocket, when I got the pack of cigarettes, under it I found something, a key, a door key . . .

She was silent, not even looking at me. Bad, mother, something very bad, perhaps I shouldn't have told you — how could I not, I would, I had to tell — a yellow brass key, mother, long, it belongs to none of the doors I know, neither in this house nor elsewhere, except one, there is one door, a door I know, the other day I held its key, I know, a key that looked as if one of its notches was broken, this one, too, mother, Tijen Hanim's key . . .

I told everything without any of the words getting caught in my throat. The other day when I went for my lesson, Tijen Hanim did not come down to open her door but threw the key from the upstairs window. She had just dyed her hair that day, and she kept pointing out my faults, I had studied the lessons but somehow she tried to improve my answers even when they were correct, she was angry, then she kissed me, don't mind me, she said, today I am a bit irritable, her lips were thick, moist, hot, and ugly, the dye smell filled my nostrils as I tried to pull my face away.

The woman who has been coming to my house for years, mother said — her voice wasn't muffled, sharp or withdrawn — coming and going for years. I didn't want her to tutor you in the first place; she has known you since you were a baby but she's man-crazy, she couldn't keep any of them yet she still melts whenever she sees one, I didn't want her to tutor you, I didn't, I was afraid for you, whereas . . . Then this means that she has done it with your father, this means the two of them have done it to me, this means they didn't have any misgivings . . . For I don't know how many months now, every so often, Reshit has come home a little late, wearing a smile, he knows I'd never ask him where he's been, but he's told me all kinds of business stories, trying to convince me that his work is improving, that it is going to improve, that we'll make a lot of money, evening after evening, for how many months, at first I thought he was out drinking, but soon I noticed his breath wasn't smelling of alcohol, this was real emotion, so I also started feeling happy, happy for you, that you would get to live a different kind of life, I thought he was coming home to drink out of joy, but it turns out . . .

No, no, it can't be, are you crazy, Mushfik, are you insane (how she kept asking me when she obviously didn't believe I was insane, she certainly couldn't have said such things during the period when I really was insane, who knows what she did then?) repent, child, don't you know that what you just said is a sin, a sin, a sin, you're slandering your father, son. Come, then, I said, come and see for yourself, then you'll know if I am making it all up or not, why do you think I stayed in the room for so long? Why did you get suspicious and come to fetch me? She couldn't stand that her intuition might be wrong, she got up from her chair with unusual agility, and we went to their room. I took the key from the pocket and handed it to her. It rested in her palm, yellow, shiny, long, one of its notches looked broken, deformed. Like all things evil. This key is that key, Mother, I said, now I could even swear that it was, but it doesn't have to mean anything, does it, Mother, besides, why start a fight now, Mother, you know the woman, maybe she gave the key to him because she needed a duplicate made, or maybe she wanted him to file the notch for her.

I was thinking of Tijen Hanim's bed, occupying more than half the space in the biggest room of her small house, a bed for two, high, wide, bulging, the bed that once belonged to her husband who ran away; I remembered the window to the right of the bed that overlooked the roofs of nearby houses—I used to love looking out that window when I was small, it pleases me even now, seeing the tops of streetcars on that narrow street, human beings rendered insignificant when seen from the sixth floor—in that bed, years ago . . .

Once when Mother and I came to Istanbul from Sarikum, we had visited Tijen Hanim, the two women had sat in the living room and talked for a long time, I had grown sleepy, Tijen Hanim had quickly picked me up in her arms, carried me to her bed, and laid me down; it was a very comfortable bed, soft, soothing. I envisioned the two of them lying on that bed: Tijen Hanim with her decrepit, solicitous embrace, my father—Reshit Bey—lying beside her, resting, conjuring the tales he'll tell his wife (Mother was now asking, was it that woman's money, was it that woman's money he thought he'd bring home, her mind still drawn toward those tales); Reshit Bey who for some time had been forgetting to give me Tijen Hanim's fee inside yellow envelopes; Tijen Hanim who waited for his arrival, ready with her hair dyed, her forehead, temples, the back of her ears, all painted; the warm, soft, slippery bed where there were no drinks, no sea, no sun, no dreams, the bed of stale hopes, the sheets the color of soiled bills, smelling of toothpaste. How come the oily, burned-dye smell never came between them?

Forget all this, Mother said, forget it, you don't have to know anything—Dilaver! his angry voice called from the outside, Dilaver, bring me some cheese, will you—you will know nothing—Dilaver, Mushfik, where in the world are you, I want some cheese, his voice was muffled, not the way it used to resonate in Sarikum, muffled so that the neighbors wouldn't hear it, so that it wouldn't reach beyond the concrete wall—I'll talk to him, no, don't be afraid, not now, tomorrow, or the day after, whenever it feels right, because I have you to worry about—I heard something shatter, echoed by the concrete walls in the yard, Mother, he wants cheese, I said, I think he's coming this way—but I will have discovered the key tonight, you don't have to worry about the rest, forget everything and go to your bed. She needed me to shield herself against Tijen Hanim. She pushed me out of the room, closed the door behind me, rushed back to the kitchen, grabbed the cheese, and took it to him before he could come inside. I was making up the boy's bed, I heard her say, he was grumbling. He sat back in his chair and stomped his feet on the ground where Hans was buried.

But pretending that I knew nothing would have amounted to betraying my father's— Reshit Bey's—righteousness. All of a sudden I remembered. I must have been around five at the time, we were visiting a neighbor's home; as the adults sat and talked, I had quietly opened the doors, wandered around the rooms. They had said nothing, knowing I wouldn't touch anything. There was a dark room I loved and wasn't scared of; despite its darkness, it had a happy side. That was the last room I entered. While walking around, I noticed a quarter on the table. Shiny, perfectly round, tempting. Knowing that I was doing something wrong, I tossed it in my pocket. Back home that evening, when I told my father what I had done, he became furious with me, you go back right away, he said, you go back and return it without delaying another moment, but my mother intervened, are you crazy, Reshit, she said, he made a mistake, he promised me he won't do anything like this ever again in his life, there is no way I'll let him go back, she said, do you want the neighbors to think that your son is a thief, that he stole money, she asked him, I'm not saying your son is a thief, he replied, but what he has done is called stealing, either he goes now and returns the money or he is in for a mean punishment, he said, I was crying, I was crying, I won't do it again, dear father, I was telling him, please don't make me go back there, if you won't go, then I will, father said and, grabbing my arm, he shoved me in my bed, slammed the door, and left, I could hear my mother pleading with him, I was ashamed for having put her through such an ordeal, please, don't go, Reshit Bey, she was saying, please don't go, think of me, not him, think of me, she was saying, trying to calm him down, then, suddenly, she asked, so it doesn't bother you that they'll think of Mushfik as a thief, is this what I'm supposed to understand, then my father's—Reshit Bey's—voice had come roaring, of course it does, of course it bothers me, wouldn't you blush when they point their finger at Mushfik and say, look at the child Reshit has raised, he asked, then, after a brief silence, fine, he said, fine, so be it, this twenty-five cents' worth of thievery may come to harm you one day, I won't live long enough to see him grown up anyway. Then the street door slammed shut. My mother came into my room, do you like what you did, she asked, only I know what I've had to go through until I was able to dissuade the wronged man. I wrapped my arms around her neck and cried. I remember saying to her, I wish you had let him go, Mother, I wish he had gone back and told them what I did, then you wouldn't have to let me in the house, then the two of you wouldn't have to fight.

I had betrayed not the man but the righteousness that was the core of his being.

Four days after the key incident, they both returned. I understood that it was over. I didn't ask Mother anything. Her eyes were red. She went to her room, laid in her bed, and cried endlessly. When I went to her, no more lessons, she said, and nothing else. Then she came out, set the table, prepared our meal, that evening my father—Reshit Bey—and I ate face to face, without Mother. Each time our eyes met, I could see bitter remorse in his eyes. But he said nothing, ever. Till the day he died. I am sure he knew who had found the key. But the man who, after a fight two months ago, went out and sat on park benches that he had never sat on before, the man who made us go from precinct to precinct to check if he had been in an accident, the man who, when found, saw me sobbing inconsolably and told me he wouldn't do it again, he wouldn't leave me again, that man did nothing, I never heard him fight with my mother again. Until the very day that death filled the house, until the day when I went to school, caring little that he needed his pills, and was summoned back to see his dead body, until that day, there was neither fighting in the house nor a sign of life . . .

I remembered all this while watching the cats; once again, Mother probably wasn't sure in what thoughts I was lost . . .

I found this tonight, while sorting through some old papers— already six months since I wrote it. Today is the 12th. Reshit Bey died ten years ago, on the 10th of this month. For eight years now, the 10th of this month comes and goes, I forget that he died on that day, I know that five years ago today they put me in the hospital, but I am beginning to forget even that, Mother feels hurt, she gets emotional when she remembers this day as well, this morning she was looking at me and remembering, whereas I just now realized what was particular about today, Mother was lost in thoughts, true, but this must not have been a day she wanted me to remember, Mother feels hurt, I know she thinks I'll forget her the same way, but she knows I won't be able to, she knows it but she still enjoys feeling hurt. Her life depends on it.

But for me, everything is over. Now there is only the one whose name precedes everything I write, the one with whom *my* life began. The rest, all else, is in the past, the inaccessible, irrecoverable past.

1957

# THE BITTER ROOT TASTING RAIN

**MUSHFIK**

After May, the soil would crack open, the emaciated weeds would begin to yellow at their stems, and the thistles, the foxtails, the mustard greens, and wild onions would thrive along the edges of the open fields. The scent of all these weeds and plants would come gushing from the cracks in the hard, scorched soil, as if to taunt the sky that felt its rainless poverty all the more intensely. In the evenings, the litany of frogs in Meryem's garden would reach our yard, the spot where my father would sit drinking his *raki*. He wouldn't hear them. My mother would lend her ear to this sea of sounds, dive into it, and swimming to the other shore, retrieve her childhood to describe it to the star-studded sky. (She'd describe the place called Derecik I saw it years later and tried in vain to find the spots that existed only in her past she'd tell me how each summer her father closed the suitcases by sitting on them and put the family on the train in Haydarpasha time stretched endlessly between departure and arrival how finally at the station when they were about to get in the cab that would take them to Derecik she always made her mother angry because she was all excited. I'd then under-stand how someone who yearned for two months' worth of life could endure everything in the other ten—the rain the mud of Istanbul the toil of studying her teachers' temper her father's con-stant love her mother's love that flared up and died down that seeped and flowed and nourished between stretches of anger her father chasing her on the streets on the day she was terrified of the smallpox vaccination everything everything she heaped together in the span of ten months—I'd then understand all that she braved with the anticipation of the two bountiful months.) We'd sit by the kitchen window. (As soon as they got to Derecik she'd leave her mother's side and run she'd run without minding her mother's anger or the onlookers she'd run even faster than the cats trying to run away from her she'd run all the way to her aunt's house and suddenly stop on reaching the first house in the alley then walk coquettishly in front of the Bamyaci's daughter who always had a runny nose she'd say to her Hey girl we're back why don't you come by our house so we can play she'd then shoot off like an arrow and wouldn't stop to catch her breath until she arrived at her aunt's. She'd go inside and call her granny who was carried on and off the train in her tiny son's arms the granny whose body came slowly down the stairs while her aunt rushed over and hugged and kissed and squeezed her. Of course her granny had no strength to do any-thing like this and a few years later my mother was strong enough to hold granny in her arms and pick her up. Once she was done kissing and hugging granny mother went to her younger aunt whom she didn't love but pitied instead her aunt whom she didn't love who secretly drank her *raki* every day and for whom both her mother and sister had lost all hope—not just for her recovery but for her self—she didn't love her because her breath stank of *raki* but still pitied her because she thought she was supposed to pity her because her aunt was the black sheep of the family because whenever they mentioned her they added the word poor before or after her name but she later learned that even she could be loved. She told all about her aunt's oily hands when she'd come out of the kitchen and try to hug and press my mother against her chest without getting her oily hands on her she used to mock her aunt until she turned twelve she used to follow her each time she saw her sneaking into the cellar she would hide in one of the corners then follow her quietly crawl closely behind almost touching her skirt and once they made it to the corner behind the mattresses her aunt's hands would reach underneath her apron inside her big pocket—and if you knew all she had inside that pocket I was always curious I would always try to put my hand inside the pocket her hand would always try to pull mine out her hand would always gently reach inside and touch mine and scare me yet the things she had in that pocket bread crumbs cork bits strings keys but I could never understand the keys since not a single door of the house was ever locked I figured out later that the keys belonged to her suit-cases inside which she kept her trousseau folded for twenty years she'd open them on days when she was full of sorrow and tears she'd go through the articles pull out the linen and hand-embroidered tablecloths by their corners sometimes wipe her tears on one then put everything back in and lock the suitcases again I knew all this well since I watched her many times through the crack in the door to the trousseau room she'd cry and cry yet all those years she refused to change her mind as I'd learn much later. She finished preparing her trousseau twenty years before just days before entering her bridal room she used to be an exceptionally meticu-lous girl and everyone in Derecik knew she loved the man she was about to marry but then the wedding day finally arrived and my young aunt said she didn't want to marry and caused quite a stir in Derecik she refused to listen to any counsel instead locked herself in her room and threatened to kill herself—I call her room the trousseau room since she did her embroidery and sewing in there and considered it hers—it turns out she dragged and set one of her suitcases against the door and threatened to kill herself if anyone tried to open the door twenty days passed like this then she quieted down and when they were able to open her door they saw my young aunt lying exhausted in the middle of the floor the suitcase holding the door laid open bread crumbs all over the linen and in one corner of the room a bunch of empty bottles jugs and cups. Evidently my young aunt had been planning this for some time but nobody could scold her instead from that day on everyone thought she was possessed. Years passed gossip died down everything was forgotten but—I still remember her epileptic seizures I witnessed a few of them with my own eyes—left behind was this girl alcoholic and possessed yes everything was forgotten with the passing years but nobody not even her mom or dad was able to figure out why she did what she did and now that it's been almost twenty-five years since she died nobody knows the real truth and nobody will besides I don't know if anyone in Derecik even remembers her—as I was saying she'd reach underneath her apron inside that big pocket she'd pull out her bottle one of her bottles to be exact and she'd drink her *raki* straight without water she had a few bottles hidden in different places she still thought her mother or sister wanted to stop her from drinking and true they did but it was too late and they knew they could do little to save her they entrusted the poor woman to God they pitied more than loved her and left her in charge of the kitchen so as I was saying her hands were always drenched in oil I still remember the taste of the meals she cooked from morning till night yes at times her oily hands would disgust me but I enjoyed no less her delicious *dolmas* her deep-fried dishes when I returned from the beach or the gardens at noon or in the evening. Often I'd tease her and catch her just when she'd be toiling among the pots and pans vegetables rice olive-oil bottles bags of flour kneading boards rolling pins and I'd ask her the time she used to have a watch with enamel settings.) That's how she would tell the story. The kitchen window would be open, its bars lined with wire netting. Sitting there, we'd watch my father through a silvery haze. At his little table between two rose bushes, my father would sip his *raki* without water and stare in front of him when slicing the sharp cheese and the sweet melon, and then stare at the sky when his mouth was empty. (Her aunt had a watch with enamel settings my mother would resume her story a beautiful watch delicate full of colors that her father my grandfather had bought for her before she went to sleep every night her aunt would wind it with care bring it to her ear and listen to it ticking then bring it to her lips and kiss it then put it inside its pouch and lay it by her head how I loved the way she handled the watch sometimes in the chaos of her kitchen I'd snuggle up to her and ask her dear auntie I'd say what time is it she'd reply it's whatever time it is what's it to you what business do you have with the time she'd say and laugh and call me my one and only then she'd extend her hands but remembering that they were oily she'd curve them up at the wrists her hands looked like little birds that flutter about on seeing a falcon in the sky so she'd hold my face with her arms and say God bless you child you couldn't find a better time to ask the time and she'd still feel happy inside — I'm certain she felt happy this was probably among the greatest joys I gave her — then while using her pinkies she'd try to undo her buttons and after much flustering labor and all the beads of sweat glowing on her forehead she'd find and pull out the cord amid the layers of shirts then still using her pinkies she'd open the pouch and bring the watch to her face as if to smell it or to press it against her cheek then she'd look at it for a long long time as if she wished that time stood still as if she wanted to eternalize the moment through memory — I often wondered if the watch had stopped as I noticed a perfect stillness in her face yet I also read time's endless passing in her face the elusive movement of the hand always toward the next digit I saw sorrow in her face as if she were grieving that after all time didn't stand still as if she felt remorse that her time wasn't up yet—then she'd use her pinkies again to put the delicate colorful watch inside its pouch then the pouch against her chest underneath the layers of shirts. Ah how could I not pity her how could I injure the dear woman.) Through the window, I'd stare at the wooden fence, and beyond it, at the top trim of Hasene Hanim's window frame, and over it, at the wood siding, and above everything, at the dark, milky blue sky studded with stars. My mother would continue. (Ah those years are gone gone one summer day granny came all the way to the station and father took her in his arms put her in the car and asked the cabby to drive she had buried her sobbing face in her handkerchief I didn't know then that we'd never come back that granny would die the following winter that the tough war years in Istanbul would make travel to Derecik unthinkable I didn't know that one perfectly ordinary evening my young aunt would drink not a sip more than her usual amount then wind her watch carefully lovingly as if worshiping it then put the watch inside the pouch lay the pouch by her head and not wake up in the morning the same year my older aunt would sell the house without even telling my father and come to live with us although we barely had enough food for the four of us. I didn't know that I'd never get to invite the Bamyacis' daughter to our house again even though her runny nose her smeared lips her unwashed chapped mucus-smeared lips disgusted me even though Mother and Granny used to get angry with me for giving her a dime so she would scratch my itchy legs but I enjoyed it so much yes I'd have either my legs or my head scratched I loved the sweet feeling and the Bamyacis' daughter used to like me and flatter me as their neighbor from the city and would die to play with me but I couldn't stand playing with that girl with the runny nose except of course on the seashore or in the vineyards when the sun made my legs itch or my long braided hair felt so heavy that I had to unbraid it and then I'd let her scratch my head. Ah the days spent in the vineyards when I'd wander from one vine to the next and satisfy my hunger by tasting one just one grape from each I'd take the path forbidden to men slip through the narrow opening between the rocks that you could block with just a few bath towels I'd descend to the seashore swim all the way to the deeper parts and make my mother yell and shriek after me yes those days never returned ever. My father and brother died in the war years and still Mother and I found in us the strength to keep on living but those days never returned ever . . .) I still can't imagine what Mother was thinking when she watched my father sitting outside, drinking. I guess there were times when she wished he were dead. As she told me the wonderful story of her childhood, I know I sensed that she was gazing at him with a bluish, silvery trembling gaze, through the wire netting and the bars on the window. That's all. To this day I can't understand why she married him. But he was a good man. (He wasn't like other fathers who brought their kids something every evening, neither would he buy what I wanted, no matter how hard I cried. And yet, quite unexpectedly, if it occurred to him that he could make me happy, then he'd buy me something right away, a magazine, candy, a balloon, or a paper flag on national holidays. Maybe I enjoyed it or I didn't, I still can't tell. Yes, there were times I wished he were dead, but just so I could be alone with Mother. Whenever he hurt me, sometimes he did hurt me, I'd wish he were dead. And perhaps not just the way other children wish from time to time; rather, I'd wish he were dead, stiff and cold, carried out of the house, never to return, I'd wish it with all my might. But I think Mother loved him, or maybe she both loved him and didn't. There were many times he hurt me, many times he hurt her, many times he hurt us, and that's when perhaps she wished he were dead, while feeling shame, knowing she was sinning, still she wished him dead. They'd fight, often they would, but the fights were not hurtful. They neither insulted each other nor used stabbing words. He was a patient man. Many times Mother berated me for not showing him the respect and love she thought he deserved. He is your father, she'd say, your father. But she never asked for as much love and respect for herself, never said, I'm your mother, your own mother. Back then I sensed nothing, of course; all this I remembered much later. And what good did remembering do?)

Then the sky would grow dark. Father would keep drinking. (Now I can call him father. I no longer feel anger or vengeance. Perhaps some bitterness. Yes, from time to time I still get upset at him for thoughtlessly taking upon himself a responsibility that would outlive him and extend through the centuries, but the feeling is not really anger as much as it is bitterness. I still can't understand how Mother could have married this man, my mother, the same woman who, one night back in the war years when her father's illness worsened, dared to go to the pharmacist's house without even batting an eye, and walked the streets where drunken foreign soldiers accosted anyone passing, in those days when the Senegalese soldiers were rumored to have bitten off a prostitute's nipple and killed her in one of the brothels. How could she have settled for him, after loving that engineer who, just a few days before their wedding, was hit by a car and lay in the middle of the road, drowning in his own blood, the man whose death she had witnessed — the man, my real father, for the first time I was seeing it clearly — and she had fainted when she could feel no pulse, how could she have? She offered me the pastry man as a father, endured him for my sake, and yet, until then, she had been able to manage a life for herself and earn money like a man back in the days when women had just started going to work. But after marrying the man and moving to Sarikum, she became the woman who sat by her window during the few hours left after her chores, dove into dreams, swam and sank deeper and deeper in the undercurrents of that sea, forever below its surface and never reaching the bottom, and even if she did, she felt no desire to muster enough strength to use her feet and spring her body back to the surface. She became the woman who never left her house; who told horror-filled fairy tales to kids my age; who accepted the nickname, "the matriarch," that was somehow invented for her. The woman who adored bearing the curse as well as the glory of being from the old world. She responded swiftly and angrily whenever I failed to show my father, Reshit Börekci, his due love and respect, even when my conduct was just a childish reaction. She was self-confident and, therefore, had no need to enforce such behavior toward herself. She had grown used to the fact that the mansion on the Bosphorus had belonged to a father who didn't mind giving his daughter to a man who had started as a scribe and risen in rank; that man who had come from Derecik was intelligent, hardworking, and loyal, but the mansion had belonged to my grandmother's father, and my mother was accustomed to matrilineal authority. As it turned out, my grandfather couldn't quite manage to run the mansion, and at the start of the war's devastation, the family had to sell it and move to the city. In the new house, first my grandfather died, then my uncle. Grandmother had shown her strength in burying the dried-out male veins of the family, but afterward it was left to my mother to fill the void, and I suppose that's how she came to savor the taste of female authority. Yet in the end, she wanted to be weak, defeated. She married him. He was a good man, but . . .) He would lean back in his chair and stretch his legs under the little drinking table. By then, the two of us would have grown silent behind the window. He never asked us to join him. Everything he needed was on the table. And the extra provisions were on the tray-table that remained hidden behind his table. Each time he leaned back, stretched his legs and we understood that he had eaten all there was to eat on the table, his arm would reach into the darkness and pull out, as if magically, a handful of cherries, grapes, or plums. Eventually I could not distinguish those fruits born out of darkness, because by then the sky would have turned pitch black and sleep would fill my eyes. My mother would pierce through her silence with a deep sigh, then, scared, or more likely, anxious, she would quickly close up the hole and squeeze my hand inside her palm. (After their fights she would come clenching her jawbones, take me in her arms and carry me to the window or to Grandmother's room, and cry quietly while pressing me against her chest. I am enduring all this for you, just for you, her words still ring in my ears. Outside, the crickets would stir up the heat trapped among the green foliage.) Already back then, I had learned to be her sole support. But she would stare at my face without knowing I had slipped away, far away, past the wooden fence, the well-crank and the rooftops, beyond Meryem's pond swarming with frogs and deep dark greens glazed by the night's silvery hue, beyond the cemetery plot under a thick fog on the outskirts of the village, even beyond the meadows that were forbidden to me and therefore I knew inch by inch. (She knew I was a dreamer, but when she dove into her own dreams and was trapped in their darkness — like a lost fish that circled around itself beating its tail frantically — she would forget me, the person who didn't like my dreaming was my father, that is, Reshit, he didn't want me to dream, he would try to keep me from dreaming, he was jealous, throughout those years, each time I saw his face, my dreams cowered, disappeared, died, he was jealous while my mother perhaps didn't even notice my dreams.) I wouldn't come back from those places completely, I would resent her for loving me without giving much thought to me. (My childhood sensitivity helped me understand a lot of things but I also misunderstood plenty . . .) I would float instead on the threshold of two worlds, stare at my father, at the man who drank his *raki* without rest or respite, neither exhausting it nor being exhausted, as if he was no longer thinking that tomorrow morning he would go to his bakery oven and distribute the *böreks* among the kids who sold them in so many different locations, or that once upon a time he had sold them himself. (When mother first arrived in Sarikum, father had only one helper, Osman the Doll Maker, may he rest in peace, but when he left, Dad worked alone, tried to run the business by himself for years; of those days, I only remember him coming home in the afternoons, exhausted, and, one time, him pulling my mother aside and excitedly telling her something, the only face I can still remember clearly, still picture vividly, is my mother's face staring at the man who overcame his exhaustion to tell her something, her face rapt, in disbelief, full of dreams. Shortly afterwards, he stopped selling his *böreks* at the train station, little kids were now selling them all over Sarikum, and that was also when he began drinking with the abandon of men whose newly found confidence quickly turns to impudence.) But when he lifted his head up to the sky (I had sensed even as a child that he was a person who dismissed everything he experienced, who forgot that he was alive and fancied instead the days yet to be lived; he had a good heart, yet he didn't love me) he was a sack held up only by dreams. Still, he didn't love me (even though he was a good man) because he couldn't fit me into his dreams. (I believe he never realized his dreams perhaps because he knew his strength would fail their vastness, it didn't even bother him to let little kids sell his pastries instead of selling them himself. Later, we survived the war, the troubles, and he never returned to his pastry business, instead he went to Istanbul to try his hand in all sorts of new ventures and failed, his dreams still ran tens of steps ahead of him, he didn't want to fit me into his dreams, he didn't want my help, yet he took it upon himself to raise me; had he perhaps asked for my help, had he been able to ask, perhaps, I, too, could have . . .) In those days, I thought about running away, without knowing why; I spent hours at my mother's knees, half-asleep, smelling the odors of distant meadows, dense, yellowing, thirsty; I gave life to the vast desert beyond my mother's longings and fattened the savage creatures of her jealousy, not knowing I'd go insane one day; and in my ignorance, I dreamed of joys that remained beyond the grasp of a greedy solitude and always returned to the sight of my father, still drinking without stop or rest, without exhaustion into the night, under the extinguishing stars.

Years later, one morning, the school principal told me that my father was gravely ill (I kept repeating, I had left him feeling a little weak but that was all, why are they calling me home? He already has his medication, I don't have to buy any, why are they calling me home?) then he signed a permission slip and sent me home, and when I saw my father with his jaw held closed by a band of gauze wrapped around his head, I felt bathed in a brilliance made of my mother's incessant sobbing. (I sensed an ancient regret in her sobbing, deep, suppressed, long forgotten, more than the sadness of death, as though she felt she had not been good to him, as though she regretted not helping him carry his dreams and had been too busy dreaming hers, perhaps she could have entered his dreams, not left him alone, she could have pushed me, forced me to get close to him, perhaps she could have, at one point in her life, but I know she didn't, I could sense even then that all her dreams revolved solely around me.) But I found the way, through the haze of emotions, not to feel anger, not to be able to feel anger toward him for drinking so much, for forgetting us and losing himself in his darkness, in his unattainable dreams, for being misunderstood, humiliated, for having played the role of a man who could never do enough to please, and for not offering my mother any being besides me whom she could hold, love, curse, feel angry toward, any flesh-and-bone pretext to keep on living. (He must have meant something since I still wonder whether I loved him or not; that night, for instance, when he left right after fighting with my mother and went to a park he had never gone to in his life—I don't remember a single night when he didn't come home—and sought solace from his wretchedness on one of the benches, the night when, after waiting for hours, Mother and I went from precinct to precinct, inquiring whether he had been in an accident and finally found him under the trees, sitting in darkness, forlorn, that night I felt neither the pain of losing him nor the joy of finding him, instead I was angry at him for trying to toy with our emotions, for knowing perfectly well the futility of his actions, but when we returned home and they went to bed, I cried, sobbing inconsolably—even on the day he died I didn't cry, I couldn't—and my sobbing woke them up, brought them to my room, he hugged me, don't cry, my son, he said, I won't do it again, I won't leave you ever, I'll always stay with you, he said and tried to stop me from crying as if mine were a mere child's tears, he stayed with me, caressed my hair—to this day I still don't know what made me cry so much that night—and yet I couldn't forgive him for what he did—why did I cry so much . . .) Father was in the past now. So were Suat and many others. The path on which I followed my heart's instinct made me quickly forget father. He was never jealous of me, except for my dreams, and even of those he really wasn't jealous, he had trusted me with everything that he had kept beyond the sealed doors of his own dreams, that is, he had trusted me beyond the realm of trust, where trust ought to have ended, where trust had no value and not even a hairline separated trust and its absence. In her own dreams, my mother stood among the ruins of trust, nursing its devastation.

My mother did not trust me, I know, I have known all along. Because we loved each other. But I trusted those I loved. I was wrong. Not because I trusted them, but because I loved incompletely, because I didn't know how to love and loved instead those who stood outside love's boundaries—like pebbles on the shore that don't belong to the sea—I loved and respected them beyond their due. I was wrong. Even now, as I think of it, I'm drowning in this wrong. Because I lose myself in this mental nitpicking.

Today, everything feels easy, after having tasted insanity, love, devastation, and recovery, after having found at last my own singular path that strikingly resembles all other paths, after having come to understand Judas in the brimming absurdity of peace. Not that I won't face difficulty from here on; rather, everything feels easy because I now know the insuperable difficulty of love.

Judas kissed Jesus when betraying him. Not out of malice but because he loved him, because he was jealous and couldn't bring himself to share him with eleven others, because he couldn't bear the thought of letting him dissolve into a dream bigger than Judas, bigger than the other eleven and even Jesus, he kissed him when betraying him because he knew it meant letting him die. Because kissing was the only thing he could think of, because he couldn't entrust his fiery love to, or blame it on, someone else, nor could he sacrifice it, as he bid farewell to Jesus who stood unknowingly on death's threshold. So he wouldn't go insane for sending him to death. Yet on the night of the kiss, as he tied the noose of breathless eternity around his neck, he was certain of Jesus' death. Because love was petty, weak, and he could hold on to nothing else; he took the sea's phosphorescent ripples for heavenly light. He couldn't trust the one who trusted him; he was jealous of him, jealous like the other one. The other one.

## RANA

I meant the world to him. He knew it, I knew he did. Until Mushfik showed up, like a scorching, desiccating August sun, like those liquids that melt everything they touch. We were comfortable, or maybe not, but we had no worries since we derived comfort from our illusion of comfort. My little qualms, occasional jealousies rolled over this illusory surface, not unlike the tiny beads of water that gently slide down the feathery backs of ducks. I meant the world to him. I and no one else had the right to his heart.

## MUSHFIK

Just like Rana. I still can't understand her. Or I am afraid to understand. Theirs is a tale founded on impossibility; whether it started in the rain or under a meadow sun, its impossible foundation would cause that impossible structure to crack at the first tremor. I am afraid to try to explain the particular tremor. It's well worth it, of course. I must try to find another loose end to untangle this jealous monopolizing love . . .

## DILAVER

He is starting to forget me again. He no longer stops by. My wish had been fulfilled. He had returned to me (he left the house five streets away, thirty-nine doors down, and returned to me one evening, he walked straight to his old room, opened the door, looked inside, and slowly closed the door, but he had clearly tamed his madness, made peace with it, and with me). I was overjoyed. I had been waiting for his return ever since he told me he'd found peace, learned to be happy. One day (I had said nothing, he was happy, I was just looking at him, at his face, his ruined face that had discovered beauty somewhere inside and was able to glow again) out of the blue (I hadn't even let him sense my wish, I didn't want to distress him, I had been acting as though I had grown used to having lost him) when he told me, mother, I'll move back in and live with you (dear God, you know, you saw that I had said nothing, done nothing, disclosed none of my sorrows, to make him utter those words) I was so overjoyed that I didn't know what to say. (I was elated, elated, I quickly forgot all those painful years, the time when he told me, Mother, can you hear the noise, the voices of all the people who don't want to die, who are running away from death, even though they must die, and while telling me these things, his frightened eyes would stare at the window, and he would hide in the corner of the room darkened by the drapes, I forgot the period that had started well before that quiet, sunny, fragrant afternoon, even before Reshit's death, the years that had begun with his odd nervousness that I first attributed to his youth then to things I couldn't understand, I was beginning to feel the dissipation of the pain that I had first experienced at his nervousness, the pain that later congealed, turned bone-hard when Reshit died, and worsened during his illness, the pain nursed by blistering shame, by insidious guilt — guilt that had sat in a remote corner of my being, that sprang like an arrow, stung, numbed, and paralyzed me — the pain that turned into poison over the years, having been distilled slowly, patiently, in an unknown still by an unknown hand.) But later, one day (no, not much later, it was the day after he had returned, but that first day had felt so long, brimming with so much) his lover visited. (I, too, know that the word, lover, is inadequate, vague, I know it, too, perhaps I can say, his friend, his companion, the way he does, I should say companion without giving it as much meaning as he does, as little thought as he does; year after year, the faces kept changing, but what Mushfik looked for in them stayed the same, he doesn't think I can understand or feel these things like he does, perhaps I should say, his companion visited.) I tried everything I could in order to receive his companion the way Mushfik wanted me to, I wanted to make him happy, to renew our old ties (time only seemed to sever them but didn't, it just weakened them, even if to

the extent of even convincing me that they were severed, the ties
that bound my hands and arms ever since I felt his heartbeat in my
womb, the ties that changed everything about my life) I wanted to
renew them (to bind him back to me, to do all that I had been
waiting, aching, dying to do in the years after his recovery when he
lived away from me, I wanted him to expect me to fulfill all his
needs and wishes, I wanted to offer my whole life back to him) I
tried to tolerate his drinking (even though it was hurting him even
though the doctors had pulled me aside—no longer showing me
the respect they once did, as if they were dealing with just any old
patient—and told me he shouldn't drink and if he must I should
make sure that he drinks very little) I tried to respect what he
wanted to eat, when he made it clear that he didn't care to see me,
when he shut himself in his room with others (I know few things
angered him as much as my entering his room when he was talking
with people he dearly loved there were times I couldn't stand his
privacy and barged into his room expecting to see something something horrible expecting to find him laying in his bed drenched in
blood but all I met was the silence of his face showering me with
anger eventually I learned to tolerate this too I no longer go in his
room I listen instead to his soft voice behind the closed door—the
softness I had forgotten over the years—I enjoy the ebb and flow
of his voice, its sweet ripples punctuated by the other's voice, the
calm murmur that flows effortlessly as if time and eternity were on
its side) I tried to respect him, did everything I could, tried to hide
in my withered bosom the empty hope that he'd ask me to tell him
a fairy tale, I asked nothing of him, dear God is my witness (nothing
nothing that might burden or provoke him) except for one thing:
to be loved (the way he used to love me), he got upset at me again
tonight, didn't say anything, didn't shout, but he was angry at me,
what can I do, I couldn't help it, wasn't it all for his own good,
he didn't tell me Talha was coming tonight, as soon as he came

home, he said he was very tired, and went to lay in his bed (for almost an hour I kept passing by his door he was staring at the ceiling he kept smiling then sulking I was afraid at first then I concluded he was remembering something who knows what but his face grew sadder and sadder he stopped smiling the pain of his thoughts stabbed me I asked myself why is he worried tonight why is he depressed) but I didn't know Talha was coming,

then he fell asleep, I wanted to go in and cover him, the cat was snuggled by his armpit, I picked up the cat, but he had already covered himself and left me with nothing else to do, I closed his door, a little later Talha arrived,

I asked him if Mushfik knew he would be coming, yes, he said, he is waiting for me, then I told him Mushfik was asleep (I can still see on Talha's face the surprise that suggested happiness at first then worry) should I wake him up, I asked (Talha is a very good young man I liked him from the start. How I wish Mushfik had always mixed with people like him, then nothing would have happened the way it did perhaps, no, dear God, no, forgive me, if this was his fate, forgive me) Talha is a very good young man, his eyes glow, his face is bright, when he laughs it's like a stream, Mushfik, too, was like this as a child but later his eyes turned darker, lines appeared across his forehead, at the corners of his mouth, nothing remained of my dear little boy, then the illness, that illness, Talha, too, has wrinkles on his face, but his throat hasn't dried out, streams still run when he laughs, Talha lowered his sky-blue eyes, please don't wake him, he said, then he went into his room, stood by his bed and just looked at him, he straightened a corner of his blanket that had slipped to the floor, I had neglected to straighten it, he gazed, extended his hand to Mushfik's face then pulled it back, his eyes were sad but his face seemed happy, he came out tiptoeing, I asked again whether he wanted me to wake up Mushfik, I knew he would say no, and that's what he said, why don't you sit and wait a little, I said, sensitive young man that he is, he sat, he wasn't really expecting that Mushfik would wake up even though he listened for him, but Mushfik wouldn't wake up now since he didn't wake up when Talha was standing by his bed, I know how much he loved him but I couldn't bring myself to wake him, besides, didn't Talha ask me not to, he sat a little while then got up and left, five to ten minutes later Mushfik opened his door, furious, his eyes were opened wide, I knew before he asked me, I told him that Talha had come and left, he frowned, I thought he would cry, I offered him my hand, he went to the bathroom and slammed the door in my face, I said, I didn't want to wake you, he said, you could have, how many times have you woken me up for a trifle, even for a nobody, I said, I asked Talha, he didn't want me to wake you, he said, you shouldn't have asked him, since when have you started asking, don't you know I would return from death for Talha, his voice coming from behind the bathroom door, I said, but Talha didn't wake you up either, he said, of course he wouldn't, he is sensitive, he wouldn't want to wake me, that was your job, then he fell silent, he put on his coat, and dashed out the door, Jealous, he was screaming, his face, his eyes were silent, Jealous, he was howling, Jealous, ah, why did I succumb to my love, to my tenderness, I upset him, I failed him again, I should have silenced my heart and awakened him (I would have disturbed his sleep but at least he wouldn't have become angry, years ago the doctors told us, anger is not good for him but neither of us paid attention, but at least he wouldn't have become angry and walked out tonight, I wouldn't have been alone again, wouldn't have made him sad, dear God, what is all this I must endure, what's my crime, my sin, what have I done in my life, dear God, why . . .)

## TALHA

I worried. We had met that morning, he didn't look sick, but I still worried. When his mother said he was fine, I was relieved. He was tired. I didn't want to wake him up. His mother insisted but I didn't let her (I didn't want to upset her I could sense she was protective of his sleep but neither could I wake him up). Had I been able to see him, I could have postponed the talk until another time. I waited a while but he didn't wake up by himself. I left. Sat at the café. The one across from their house. Waited for him to dash out their door. I let my coffee get cold, drank it slowly. My eyes were fixed on their door. He didn't come out. I got up, returned home, regretting that I hadn't woken him up . . .

## MUSHFIK

Out of breath, I recalled all these memories when I took the shortcut through the vacant lot. How I remembered without intending to, how everything came back to me! Suddenly, I saw Sarikum's soil in the soil under my feet; it was parched, the weeds were beginning to yellow at the base. In the glow of the night, I could discern their yellowness. They gave off a sharp odor, free of rancor, free of jealousy. Little by little, my anger died down as I recalled the names of those who had hurt me with their jealousy. This way, I was going to him cleansed. My anger died down. None of them were whole. I must go to him ever more whole, ever more complete. He is complete; I am complete with him.

It was wrong to trust Mother. I didn't expect this petty act of jealousy from her but I should have known better. I am still full of sleep.

## TALHA

His eyes were wide open, fighting off sleep, when he appeared at the door. His tongue stuttered among tangled emotions. Why did you do it, he asked. That was the first thing he said. Why did you do it, you had no right, he said. I looked at his face (with the weight of all the words I silenced, I looked at his face and started to feel happy). Clearly, he was trying to look into my eyes. I waited for you all day, how could you not wake me up, don't do it again, he said. I nodded. I could feel the burning in his eyes (caught as I was in the state he called two beings become one, my eyes burned with the burning of his eyes; I wanted him to remain quiet but he kept talking, albeit haltingly, there was no end to the stream of words) I got very angry at my mother, he said, don't talk like that, I said, it saddens me, I am already sorry I didn't wake you, mind your own business, he said, squeezing my arm (he still couldn't stop talking but in his agitated state, "mind your own business" was the most he could say, I understood what he meant, I would mind my own business since that's what he has wanted all along; an incredible passion kept his mouth going while he squeezed my arm; that's all he could do, when words began losing their strength) we both fell silent. Don't do it again, you have no right, he repeated. We stared at each other sternly, then softly. Then he left. Disappeared into the darkness. Yet, I am comfortable, I am.

**MUSHFIK**

At least, Judas seems to have behaved like a man.

**RANA**

He passed me on the road this afternoon but didn't see me. I know how absorbed he gets sometimes. Still, for a moment, I felt as if he was trying to avoid me. I was upset but not for long. I had done what I was supposed to do. I don't think he avoided me, I am pretty certain now; in any case, had we not made it clear a few nights ago that it was all over? Otherwise, why would I have played the trump card and hit him with that man called Talha? I was angry, I wanted him to be angry too, but once I played that last card, I should have known that I had given up on winning. Didn't I know it, anyway? I had lost control of the game a long time ago, the day I ran into him on the street, after his period of absence. What does it matter that I had planned everything carefully and with so much anticipation? I should have known that at some point I would lose control of the game. Now all I can do is hate him, stab him in the back. But I can't even decide whether or not I should. From here on, I'll be jealous not for my happiness, my husband, my love, but I'll be jealous for him. He knows this, too. I should give up.

And how happy we were until the day he appeared. How we awaited his arrival. Sadun and he knew each other; they had met once. Sadun had often talked about him, but they didn't correspond for a long time. I wish they never had. Then Sadun started to write, and the story began. One night we came home and found him at the door. That night, the night after that, the one after that—nights followed one another, turned into weeks, then months—they loved each other. I became jealous, unbearably jealous. All of us participated in the game I invented to pry him away from the house. Even he played a part. Unknowingly. I managed to push him away, but he returned. He couldn't live without Sadun. I understood. I had to capture Sadun back. Like water, he seeped into our midst. The duck feathers began soaking up the water. If Sadun was to be mine, something about Mushfik, a flaw, had to come out in the open. And it did. To be exact, I brought it out . . .

## SADUN

What's with her again tonight? For an hour, she's been playing with the radio dials, now turning one then the other, obviously her mind is elsewhere. Yet it wasn't supposed to be like this. Her fire has died out, her womb is astir, growing, from now on it will be noticeable to everyone. Just as she wanted. She won't leave the world unnoticed (that great passion of hers fulfilled, she has achieved the sanctity of women who leave their mark in the world) everyone will respect her (she won't feel their judgment every time she looks at their faces, she will stand proudly against the world that wishes to crush the barren), even better, the child will be mine, the child will bind me to her, keep me at her side. Never mind that she has seen how even children may not keep a man from leaving his wife. She has seen it and tried to use it against Mushfik, to stab him in the back. At any rate, all that is behind us now. And everything else that has happened since then. Mushfik somehow showed up on New Year's Eve, but a week or two later, he stopped coming altogether. He probably realized the futility of his attempt. He understood that he would never get along with her (as if there was ever an indication otherwise, he should have known it all along, he wanted to try but helped nobody). Besides, during his last visit, Rana infuriated him again, it was obvious. And he responded by mocking her. Neither of them considered my feelings that night (even though both insisted they loved me neither one nor the other bothered to notice me as always I stayed out of their fight even though I was the cause of it I am condemned to stay out I don't even care let them pull and tear the blanket whichever way they want I have no say I am the blanket all this is nonsense of course I know I am making all this up to amuse myself to forgive myself but that's me I can't help this coldness I didn't ask to be loved maybe Rana loved my coldness but Mushfik expected something else from me I knew but let them let them think of me as cold unfeeling I will stay out of it even though I am the cause but that evening neither of them bothered to think of me). Caught between the silent wife and the scornful friend, my place was, as always, uncertain, a void. We talked then he left. And never showed up again. I can't even say if we saw each other on the street, that is, I don't remember, it's best for me to have forgotten. I didn't look for him, either. At first I wanted to avoid confrontation with Rana. But now, whether I look him up or not (Rana had her fill of confrontations with me, we could say they no longer hold much meaning) I know nothing will change. It's in the past. From now on, Rana will have to think of only one thing, the life growing inside her (inside her belly, in a place neither her love for me nor her hatred for others could disturb, in the fathomless depths of her belly). She has no accounts left to settle with anyone. I shouldered everything (every word every move every thought no matter from whom where or when). I no longer concern her either. Yet there's something about those radio dials. What is it that she hasn't figured out still? (tonight she will turn her back again remain silent again think again smoke again frown again even though I bet my life that I am not her preoccupation she will act as if she is angry with me as if all is not over I know I await)

## MUSHFIK

How could Rana have done this? I can think of two reasons. Either she was jealous of Sadun, or she loved me — rather, I should say, she became obsessed with me.

Why be jealous of Sadun? Sadun was hers, no one could steal him. Besides, she watched him like a hawk. Why she was afraid, why and how she wore him out, I can't tell. She is not the first wife to shoulder her husband's burden (no, I should say, she doesn't leave any burden for her husband to carry, she doesn't speak for her silent husband perhaps because she doesn't leave anything for him to say — I now remember, it was Sadun who used the term, shouldering the husband's burden — he remains silent because she says everything before she lets him speak. They don't mean to be hurtful, either the silent one or the one doing all the talking. Sadun

lets Rana nurse him, they are like a child and his jealous mother)
of course, Rana is not the first woman to shoulder this burden, neither is it fair to say she wore him out, perhaps Sadun was ready to
capitulate with all his being, or Rana prepared him to capitulate.
That Sadun could love me (could it be called love) that he could
enjoy my presence (maybe or maybe not) . . . Could Rana's husband never love anyone in his life? Never enjoy anyone's company?
Did he have to spend his every living moment for his wife (he did,
and Rana obviously asked for more) was hers the only life allowed
to intersect with his? Did Rana ever think what she would do with
Sadun once she alienated everyone else from his life?

The air is quite chilly, I am beginning to feel cold. It's damp
underneath the trees. I hope no one comes to sit on my bench (in
the dark, one quickly gets used to one's place). I don't wish to talk
right now (my head is a jumble all kinds of nonsense pass through
my mind still I'd rather not talk).

How can I forgive her for insulting Talha? Forgiveness is not
the issue; how can I ignore it, even for Sadun's sake (for his sake
because I truly loved Sadun I still think of him the man with the
mute cold placid smile who seemed distant and could get close to
no one). After all her malice . . .

(the fellow who came and sat next to me made me dizzy, he
forced himself on me, forced his conversation on me, forced me to
talk, and in the end forced himself to leave, I learned that he loved
talking with anyone just to escape the night the darkness the loneliness and the anguish I learned that he was an outcast this evening
because he got angry at his younger brother and beat him up even
though they had only each other in this life and yet they often infuriated each other I learned that when his brother dared to disrespect
him he lost his temper and slapped him in the face and now he was
burning with remorse and wanted to return home but instead
would wander under the trees and wait until his brother was asleep,

I learned all that, all that I would soon forget) I shouldn't stay here—never mind thinking straight, I can't even keep memories straight.

I'm tired.

Soon I won't wander in the night, they'll force me to follow the doctor's orders (not that I need anyone to force me my own fear will force me I know) already it's been a long time since I lost the darkness, and for a long time to come, the darkness will belong to others. I'll have no share of it.

Talha.

What is Talha doing now?

## TALHA

Everyone fell asleep. I couldn't. Darkness lives still (an immeasurable vast simmering darkness). Everyone's breathing is soft, tranquil like sleep. The dark hum undulates, follows the rhythm of breaths, rising, falling, endlessly, tirelessly (immeasurable simmering). Darkness hasn't died yet, it still lives in its own crowded company, it won't let me sleep, won't let me die. Where is Mushfik now? It's only eleven-thirty. At least two more hours before he goes to sleep. Is he working? Perhaps trying to while away the darkness. One of his last . . . (I feel I too will lose the darkness his darkness that he loved lost found and would lose again) perhaps I can see him if I go out, but I'd rather not, I don't want to see anyone. I can walk to his house since I know he isn't there. Tomorrow when I tell him I went out, he'll probably ask me if I stopped by. I'll say, no, I didn't. So that he doesn't have to regret that I couldn't find him. If I go out . . .

## GULAY

Standing at the edge of the darkness, Father was dressing. Light entered through the window. His glasses shone, like the scary man in the movie but I wasn't scared since I knew he was my father. He put his clothes on quietly, then looked at me. I closed my eyes. When I opened them, the street door closed. Where did he go? What if the scary man in the movie came when my father was gone? Afraid, I coiled under the blanket. Then the street door opened and closed. I heard my father taking off his shoes. The room had grown a little brighter. The sky's darkness was dissolving. Father again looked at me while taking off his clothes. My hair was hiding my eyes, so I didn't close them this time. Father looked tired. He sat and smoked a cigarette. I love the way the smoke takes the color of his eyes and spreads it across his face and around, but this time I couldn't make out the color. Then Father put out his cigarette and went to bed. No one woke up, no one knows beside me that my father left and returned.

## MUSHFIK

One day, before I knew that blue was the color he loved, I unexpectedly likened him to a deep arresting shade of blue in a painting, no, I didn't liken him, I said, you are this blue; at first he didn't respond but he spoke later. That blue cannot know death, it would be repulsed if it came upon death, it would toss and strain restlessly until it rids existence of death, saving only the seeds of life. Talha is life even in the midst of his defeat, he has sown his seed, he has children, he has a son who will not desert him on his deathbed, a son who will not try to turn a deaf ear to his moaning and run out of the house (I still bear the burden of my guilt); in the fathomless blue, Talha knows, senses, hopes, he won't be left alone; if he loses sleep, I know he loses it on account of this, he is afraid of choosing, of having chosen, his life over the life of his children, he wants to torment himself in order to pay for what he thinks is a crime, yet all this anxiety is in vain, all this exhausting ordeal of thinking that he has failed to meet his duties by distinguishing between his life and his duties, all in vain, he would know this, too, if he could break the habit of self-criticism and self-loathing, if he could resist internalizing defeat, surrender, if he could resist—because this blue internalizes all this just so it can torment him—he thinks he has wronged his children, his home, whereas his seed has already started sprouting, he knows he won't be left alone (the way Reshit was left alone only I know that he was abandoned at his death only I know that I abandoned him on his deathbed as if I had stopped grieving before his death . . . Only I know that I ran away from his moans but returned to find the walls still echoing with them as he laid there with his jaw held closed by a band of gauze wrapped around his head only I know that I laid in his bed after my mother was exhausted from crying and fell asleep I laid in the bed that still bore his body's impression and I searched its boundaries with my hands with my feet. Snores came from the interior of the house, the snores of the other, alien side of the family that had somehow reunited after eighteen years—how after what manner of searching and why I still can't comprehend—the snores of my aunt and her husband who pretending to help us had descended upon our house like crows on a carcass when they knew perfectly well that they had already taken everything we owned. When we moved back to Istanbul, after years without any communication, my mother's sister and her husband had suddenly appeared and tried to claim a corner of the house for themselves; they never left us alone and they became my punishment for having abandoned him in his deathbed; my aunt stood next to me by his coffin and told me that if I considered myself his son then I should behave like his son; she said these words with perfectly dry eyes and then she resumed her weeping . . . Talha's children will have no aunt like her). Talha knows all this but when it comes to tormenting himself (he knows dear God he must know that his own son will not grab the shovel and—seized with an incomprehensible rage—push the clay soil loosened by the rain so that the clumps of mud fell on the hard wooden planks with dry thuds he must know that his own son will not push back the memory of his father somewhere that anger cannot reach somewhere irretrievably distant dear God he should know) he still can't help . . .

My mind is still with him, I wonder what he is doing.

## TALHA

One day he started talking about loaves of rye bread. At first I didn't understand what rye bread stood for. Nor did I ask. He would explain it anyway. "A very strange thing occurred to me." I expected him to start telling me again about Pitkhanas of Kussara or some other name like that. I had grown used to his habit of suddenly bringing up strange, ancient figures, kings from unknown times. But these loaves of rye bread did not stand for ancient people. Much less for kings. They stood for excuses—those that had given his life direction—insignificant in themselves but destructive in their consequences.

Another time, he was talking about an old friend and he said, "Talha, in the past, in some distant stretch of my life, I came to know people through passion, through excitement. I seized, I was seized, I swept them away, I was swept away by them." I felt a pang. I wanted to think that our encounter was also born out of passion. Before I could say anything, he continued, as if sensing my thoughts, "I have felt alive in this also, I am not saying I have not given my being to this, but in the past I knew how it felt to be alone. All by myself. We weren't two people. I was one. Left alone. Lives flowed separately. Passion died out. Only a sediment remained, slowly crumbling, dissolving. Then my stream would seek another stream." I was trying to think as he spoke. The first time we met, my mind was slightly foggy. I was anxious about being brought to his house. I wasn't sure if his greeting was meant for me—there were others besides us—or if he was being a good host. "I would seek and find, I would become a machine that ignited and quenched excitement, passion."

I walked for hours, I was tired (I did all I could to tire myself I walked all the way to his house I counted the windows full of sleep I hoped we'd run into each other I hoped we wouldn't I counted the street lamps I lost count of them and gradually I realized that I had entered a blind street I walked dreading resenting hating the sidewalks the lights the crowds that in a few hours would fill up the streets I walked shuffling my feet and thinking with every step that I should walk away from everything and keep to myself again alone and withered) I tried to weigh and sort these thoughts as I walked but my mind resisted order, jumping from one thought to another (in the darkness the immeasurable simmering darkness). Now I lie in my bed, more wakeful than sleepy. I feel tired. The day is about to break. I feel tired (my legs my hands my tense overwrought forehead my strained eyes my shoulders feel as tired as if I had carried an immense weight but my mind is still racing resisting death) I have to get up in the morning and go to work. Everyone is asleep but soon sleep will become lighter. I ought to try and fall asleep right away (to die to die for the night). But for a moment I feel I am outside the machine, the cogwheels, no longer a screw. I must cleanse myself, no matter what. "I become a machine," he had said. (just when I was thinking of the day we met . . . how he had suddenly come and sat beside me and talked to me, ignoring the others, his hostly obligations, at first we talked about the only thing he knew about me . . . my poetry . . . later when I was sitting somewhere else in the room, he came over again, I don't know why but I found myself telling him—I felt that I had to tell him—about Lerzan and the children; I couldn't exactly read his reaction, I still can't, even if I tried to explain it to myself, by now I have a sense of what he'd meant, and I am not wrong, I know I am not wrong. Perhaps that very moment blocked the path of passion, when, all of a sudden, he assumed an air of overconfidence, his voice sounded sharper, and we began drinking even more. The other guests were as present as absent. Then we parted—I remember a warm sensation coursing down my body like a sweet ageless stream born in the beginning of time I had wanted it to rain that evening I had wanted the rain to stream down my hair and my face but it was snowing instead it had snowed all day and it was snowing even more heavily giving way to a slow deep freeze—that night the others decided that the two of us ought to get together again, I hesitated at first—perhaps I felt the terror introduced by the prospect of happiness perhaps I thought that drinking from the sweet stream would only increase thirst—I couldn't make up my mind. The evening when we finally met, much later than we had intended, he seemed blind to anyone else.)

Sighs come to me through the dim light, the breathing, the sudden turns, the aimless exertion, the panting, all that signals the approaching end of sleep. I have little time left. The wall has grown noticeably brighter.

(that night he had been circling around me in order to talk, as if annoyed by everything other than me, his demeanor had bothered me; whenever I saw him sit alone and drink as if to deafen himself to all the voices, I would walk up to him and put my hand on his shoulder so we could resume our conversation—he knew what the hand meant, my pleasure felt like a sweet ageless stream born in the beginning of time, his shoulder came alive under my hand, his eyes knew how to look deeply into my eyes, I felt happy as if having reached at long last the end of a vast killing frost—and we would begin talking again; at one point, he had to step away and asked me to please wait, of course I would wait but I didn't know why . . . later, on his return, time began moving again)

(why won't this light stop growing brighter, dear God)

hours passed, we went out to the street and walked, he knew—and made it known—perfectly well that he had offended the other guests, the snow had stopped some time ago, the ground was frozen, my feet were cold, he had buried his head inside his collar, soon we stopped feeling the cold, could no longer feel our feet, he pointed this out, I concurred, that was all. We were pleased to discover that we had to walk down the same street to get home; I showed him my house but instead of going in I continued on to the next street with him, there, I asked to kiss him, we kissed, he was not unwilling but reluctant. Now I understand why, he was afraid of excitement, of passion, he left, we promised each other to meet again, I looked back, he walked away without looking . . .

(the light is growing brighter, I must leave, it seems)

(but one evening) one evening, "you were ready to find me, to find in me everything you had been searching for (no no that's not quite right) "ready to find everything you have found . . ."

## GULAY

I woke up, got out of bed and quietly looked through the door, my father's hands were clasped; then his eyes closed, his hands opened, dropped. I went to the bathroom. When I returned he was sleeping, maybe snoring but it sounded more like moaning. I went back to bed. The sun is about to rise, soon they'll wake me up to send me to school. But I'll pretend I am asleep when they come. Let them work hard to wake me up. I'll go to school anyhow, and it's not that I am lazy . . .

## RANA

Last night's sleep wasn't much like sleep. I tossed and turned in bed. The one inside my belly kept moving, kicking (I love him all the more when he moves inside me, when he gives me pain, my heart feels as though it will stop but then I flow through the pain like fine flour through a sifter, and return to light, to abundance, that's when I love him the most). Sadun didn't say anything, not a word (not that I expected he would, but still . . .) but he probably sensed something, or thought he sensed. He turned his back and fell asleep (he is convinced that turning his back and falling asleep is the easiest solution, he withdraws from everything, disappears, I can't say he doesn't care, I know him well but I wish I were like him, I wish I could turn my back against the whole world, just like he does, yet without freeing myself from pain, from the feeling of being skinned alive). I still can't relax, I get all the more nervous thinking that my anxiety will be noticed. What's worse, this morning I found seven new spreadsheets on my desk. I wasn't expecting them. I am trying to work but I can't. (this all-consuming anxiety . . . now and then — no — I should say often I feel a yearning to escape I know I can escape whenever wherever I want, I know, but how do I escape this yearning to be forever elsewhere forever farther away I want to travel to remote places where the inhabitants are not my own people where they are entirely strange entirely unknown I want to be among people whose tongues habits customs I don't know even if I have to be a total stranger among them — as if I am not already a stranger here as if my father mother my husband aren't total strangers to me who I ask who among them understands me who stands by me and recognizes my struggle to salvage my pride who abstains from calling me an egotistical monster to this day) I should smoke as an excuse to take a break, otherwise I'll suffocate here. Aren't all my friends also using excuses to escape? (but when I do it it's not the same I know there is something about me that annoys people; maybe what annoys them is that I don't mind if I annoy; anyway, those who can't stand me will talk behind my back, it can't be helped. I want to leave. Perhaps it's my blood that lures me toward faraway places I hear strange places calling me places I have never seen nor even imagined places unknown to my mother or her mother a land where dark-skinned women and men with black hair wander among the mountain passes or perhaps my thinking is all wrong since I know that even if I travel there I will begin spinning my cocoon again—the inescapable cocoon of torment and venom—at the moment I break out of the old one and breathe in the pure unbearable air I will again begin spinning the cocoon that has incubated and nourished my destiny of one cursed at birth I will spin and close myself inside I will distill my torment and brew venom to destroy my enemies I will mix and stir unheard-of elements in this venom and one day I will break through the walls and come out I will be overwhelmed and lose myself then all of a sudden I will recover and want to escape again I will want to see different people experience different customs without having to ever go back to my cocoon but I know I will have enemies who will not let me live my life I will neither forgive them nor run away because even if I run away—to the place the name of which I can barely imagine the land where strange dark-skinned people wander among the mountain passes among steep sharp rocks—I know I will begin spinning my cocoon anew seized by the inevitable shame of having escaped I was born to spin this cocoon I was born to be God's black curse I can't feel alive unless I turn my torment my venom into this cocoon and seek refuge inside—just as others can't feel alive unless they love burn or destroy . . .)

I finished my cigarette and started another one without being noticed. I am thinking of those who refuse to live, who cannot live, without love, and he comes to mind. Months ago when he suddenly appeared, he stared and stared at me, obviously weighing whether or not he should turn his face away, I helped him out by saying hello. Again the devil egged me on. I didn't know what he would do, but I was curious, wondered if I was right about him.

Would he destroy my hopes? (I know the futility of mentioning hope after all that happened but I still seem to be nursing some hope inside.) "Hi," he said; I wanted him to add, "Rana," I was waiting, hoping, to hear him say my name, but the hope proved futile (which meant I could renew my enmity). I asked about him, about his mother, he, in turn, asked about me, about Sadun. I was beginning to feel rage. (Out of habit, really, otherwise there was nothing to justify my rage. If anything, I would have had to feel enraged at myself: the plot was just starting to unfold, he hadn't yet committed his error or shown his true nature.) When the game playing seemed to have gone on too long, I blurted out, "We'd like to see you again" (I couldn't hold back, I simply couldn't, I was asking for trouble). "What do you mean?" he asked with his large lips. He knew what I meant but wanted to hear me say it, pour my venom again. "At our house," I said, "we'd like to see you again, we want your friendship, the way it used to be" (knowing it could never be the same). I looked straight into his eyes, "If you can forgive me . . ." I knew his voice would break, his eyebrows would rise and his lips would curve in pain. All of which happened. "No need to talk about forgiveness," he said, "besides, I don't know what there is to forgive, I mean, there is nothing to forgive," (his eyebrows startled, his lips curved, pained) "forgiveness doesn't mean anything." I insisted, "Don't deny you were angry, you were very angry at me, and you were right." His voice became stern, "My anger is another matter, let's leave that aside," then sounding timid: "You want me to come to your home . . . again?" "Yes," I said, "that is, if you want to. But before you do, I want to talk. You can't tell Sadun that you talked to me though. I think it'd be best if you didn't." He weighed my words again; again he gave in. "If it's for his good," he said. He was pleased that he could say there was no enmity left between us. I was pleased too, the way one feels an aching pleasure when peeling the scab off an old wound.

I described Sadun's state of mind because I felt I had to tell him something; I even said, "What can I do, I will never learn," because I knew he would let down his defenses. "You'll probably be angry at what I'll say," he replied, "probably even hate me, but since you're still able to think of me as your friend, I have to speak. This sort of jealousy will get you nowhere, Rana. You should give it up. You may wish you were the only person in a man's life, but you can't succeed" (he spoke as if he understood a great deal yet at the same time as if he knew little). "It's true, you're a woman, but a man needs more," he said. "You can be his friend but you also need to respect the other people in his life. I'm sorry, but that's the way it is." I was mad now, livid. I still can't forget those words. "No, I'm not angry, not at all," I said. "I wanted to talk because I believe you're sincere. I'm listening. I can't be angry with you." How didn't I see what was coming, how didn't I anticipate his retort: "Well, what if you were angry? We lost everything we had a long time ago. Starting over is your idea," he said, he meant, with every gesture of his being. I was lost in my game, buried in my cocoon. But he was also sinking, he just hadn't noticed. Then, he said, "Even if it is for Sadun's good, it feels like a betrayal of sorts . . ."

No, the truth is, I wanted to tell him some things. I invited him to the house where life had become unbearable. Once Mushfik was out of the picture, Sadun's behavior had begun to change. Not because Mushfik left, I know. But it served as an excuse. He changed. In the past, he would tell me about his moods and I wouldn't believe him, but now I see; he became lazy, temperamental, he stopped talking to me, seemed to forget me altogether, and, from morning till night, he gave himself entirely to his books and writing. I worried about his health, but I realized later that he was taking his columns to the newspaper when I wasn't home, that he was enjoying the fresh air and returning, and it seemed like he didn't want me to know. He was being cruel to me, and I had no idea that he could be such a mean beast. Worse yet, he treated me as if I were the beast. One time, I couldn't take it any-more and left the house, that's the day I saw Mushfik. That's why I called Mushfik back, so that the two can meet and talk again, as in the past (it couldn't be as in the past for me, but perhaps it could be for Sadun, I'd thought) so that he could open his mouth and bring the old Sadun back to life. Because of this, because of Sadun, I invited him, I endured his words. Because I still loved Sadun, because I still felt jealous. I played with fire but I prevailed (the way pain prevails, the way the long-sought-after trouble prevails . . .)

I don't know how long it's been since I finished my second cigarette; they're staring at me, I should act busy, look through the spreadsheets; they shouldn't notice, I should work.


## TALHA

I opened the window. I usually find it open. But this morning I arrived early, so I opened it. Last night I must have finally fallen asleep, and when I woke up, I washed myself, put on my clothes and left. The streets were still empty. I don't feel tired. I keep losing myself in the blue outside the window then returning to the papers on my desk. Today the window is all mine, it seems. Sheets of paper pass through the machine and slowly get filled. The window opens to a blue joy that extends beyond the papers. The sheets get filled slowly, I take them out, put more in, and they, too, get filled. The blue outside the window remains in place, like joy. I wrap myself in this blue. The sky is clear, perfectly clear. My sky, my joy that I wrap myself in . . .

While falling asleep last night, I suddenly left behind the people whom Mushfik had known through excitement, through passion. I thought about us instead. I know now that it wasn't pas-sion or excitement that brought us together. We constantly felt excited but we also constantly quelled our excitement. Having neither talked nor thought about this affair, we were both frightened, and we did everything in our power not to be swept away by it. Perhaps I am happy today because of this, quietly happy, unwittingly. As he said, from the start we avoided becoming a machine, a machine of blind love. One of the first evenings together, I told him that if someone I loved wanted or liked something then I would want or like the same thing, but he disagreed right away; it's a beautiful thought, he said, but it shouldn't be that way. Quelling the excitement. Much later, one day he told me, you either love a person or you don't, but when you do, you must love him entirely, with all his flaws and deficiencies. This time it was my turn to disagree; I asked him, shouldn't the beloved have the right to try and mend these flaws and deficiencies? Without hesitation, he replied: "That would be the highest measure of love imaginable between two people."

The sky was clear blue that day also. I pretended not to have noticed his eyes fill with tears. I turned my face away, too.

Another sheet of paper.

We both sought refuge in God.

(yet I too know the desire to escape know the devastation of escape know the place the time when blue turns into yellow turns into desert I too experienced falling into the spider's web — away or in my own house near or far from my loved ones — first being stung and paralyzed then being sucked and drained of life but now I want to forget I know I am caught but I can free myself and if I am caught again and again it's neither because I try to escape nor because I am scared it's because I remember my own weaknesses. Empty words. There is the blue in front of me, there is the window . . .)

## GULAY

Now I've figured it out. Father must have gone to Uncle Mushfik last night. The teacher is looking.

## LERZAN

They can't call me lazy. I've been working since morning. The project is nearly finished. I can rest a little. Even loaf around if I want to. When I woke up in the middle of last night, Talha wasn't next to me and I got worried. I waited; no sound came from anywhere in the house. I figured he must have left. It's his habit to go out in the middle of the night. It *used to be* his habit, that is. Since Mushfik has been around, Talha has gone out only once or twice. I wondered what had happened, but then I remembered that earlier in the evening Mushfik had appeared at our door—he was out of breath—and afterwards I could tell that Talha was in a bad mood. I must have fallen asleep again. But this morning I suddenly remembered Mushfik's first visit to our house. Maybe because he was out of breath then too, and had asked if Talha was home. No, I told him, he was supposed to meet a friend at six-thirty. I am the friend, he said. I was late by five minutes and didn't find him at the bus stop. I came to ask if he didn't wait, or forgot, or decided not to come at all. What a shame, I said, he must be very sorry to have missed you too; would you care to come in and wait, although I'm not sure if he'll return, it's good that you knew where we live, I said. Yes, he showed me the other night, he said. Just then, we heard Talha's footsteps coming up the stairs. Here he is, we both said. Then the two of them sat together for a while, and later he took Talha to his house. Not long after that first visit, Mushfik began to visit regularly, he became another man in the house. I often wonder whether Talha wouldn't have waited a little longer at the bus stop that evening, had he anticipated the course of events. In any case, what happened was bound to happen.

One evening I told him how pleased I was; ever since Talha and you became friends, I told him, he has stopped hanging out with all the wrong people and drinking like he used to. But we drink too, he said; it's not the same, I said. He understood, and remained silent. I continued, he said nothing else. But clearly he was happy. I could see it in his eyes.

Then one day I began feeling depressed. Something like jealousy.

Yes, sir, it's finished, I'll bring it right away. I'm done. (I won't be able to think . . .)

## RANA

(trouble sought trouble found, as good as water, as good as air . . .)

## SADUN

There is something about today. Last night while watching Rana I was thinking of him, this morning I thought of him again, and at noon, when I saw him walking down our street, passing by our window, I thought he would stop by. I was tense with anticipation. But the doorbell didn't ring. I remembered that Talha lives three streets up from us. My breath stung in my throat (like chloroform I still can't forget the day when my high school classmates played a joke on me with a tube they held to my nose and asked me to smell I didn't know what was in it besides I considered them best friends it felt as though my lungs were being ripped open I thought I would spit blood the smell stayed with me even after I recovered I didn't try to punish my friends didn't fight them or stop talking to them just like today I was neither cross with him nor . . . what's the point . . . but I felt as if I smelled chloroform again an acid piercing sensation.) I know he'd like to come, but he won't because of Rana.

Besides, his two visits before my birthday didn't go well. I tried getting him to hurry and leave before Rana returned, but he displayed an odd sort of resistance, as if he wanted to confront Rana. I dreaded any meeting between them. I knew that Rana would say something or insult him by saying nothing at all. The last time he left, he told me not to feel sad, that he would be back (he was mocking me, he had already made up his mind, he wasn't even trying to comfort me, instead he meant to say, struggle as much as you want, I'll do whatever I want). He did come back (yet in retrospect I'm beginning to think that he came back because Rana wanted him to, maybe I am mistaken but the first time he came, that is, right after he ran into Rana, I couldn't fail to notice their strange demeanor, Rana seemed as though she had won a fight, at first I thought that perhaps Mushfik actually enjoyed her gloating and that she was happy Mushfik came back so she could prove her superiority once again, but gradually I began to discern in her winner's pride a different kind of happiness also, one that derived from no longer having to wonder whether or not what she wanted, what she yearned for, would ever materialize, I'm not sure, I'm not sure). Rana and I sat across from each other. I remembered my birthday party the year before. Many people had come to our house that night, and Mushfik was among them. The entertainment had lasted for hours (I entertained myself by watching the guests, I couldn't participate, yet I wasn't bored either, Rana knew me and still had tried everything she could in order to include me in the party but I was satisfied, I was incapable of taking any more than my own little entertainment, that's how I was, that's how I am). But something wasn't right about Rana; more precisely, after midnight she had started to behave strangely—like those sinister underground streams that flow slowly, steadily, and eventually cause the ground to collapse. The next day, her annoyance surfaced. Mushfik's name had been mixed up in a divorce story, and Rana seemed to have found what she'd been looking for. (Rather, I should say, someone had brought up Mushfik's name in connection with the story, although why Rana had been looking for this, I can't tell.) She kept repeating that Mushfik was the kind of man who wouldn't hesitate to destroy a family. (Couldn't Rana have found a better excuse, if she wanted? That's why I don't understand her behavior, worse yet, on my birthday. Mushfik never destroyed a home, nor did he harbor any such intentions.) This was all about Rana's own fears. She seemed to think that he would bring bad luck on us just because his name was mixed up in the story. Rana was jealous of me, I knew, she was afraid of losing me. That night she must have decided that Mushfik was the bearer of bad luck. She wanted to use the accusation to force him out, I realized, she didn't even want to lay eyes on him any more. She was afraid. Or she had other worries. Perhaps she was afraid of being abandoned, that I would run away. She used Mushfik as a way to confront her fears. During his next few visits, she greeted him halfheartedly, declined to talk, sulked, and finally one night she forced me to do it (if I truly didn't want to do it, if I hadn't said yes, if I hadn't said I would do it, I could have resisted; instead I did it, I must have wanted it myself, I must have thought Rana was right somehow). The next day, I felt obligated to explain everything to Mushfik. That Rana no longer trusted him; that she thought he was knowingly, willingly coming between a husband and wife; that she could no longer stand seeing him; that it would be best if he stopped coming to the house at least for a while. I was talking as if I were fleeing, as if I were being driven away. I was running away. From myself. I didn't want trouble. Mushfik understood everything readily and even tried to help me. I was ashamed, still running when Mushfik said, "Agreed, then I won't come," in a drowned voice. Only he asked to know one thing. How would we act if we saw each other on the street? It would depend, I told him. "Agreed to that, too," he said. He would still like to see me from time to time, he told me, I should visit him at his house or meet him somewhere else. I agreed, although I didn't believe it would happen. I was still running away. Farewell, I'll be waiting for your phone call, he said. But I never called. A couple of times afterwards, he visited secretly, we sat, talked, and he left. I am still amazed that I did this.

Then on my birthday, he reappeared at the door. I was surprised. He came in, greeted Rana as if nothing had happened. He sat. Briefly. Then he got up and left, saying he would visit again. I was perplexed. Rana seemed happy that he'd come. Perhaps the passing of time has changed her, I thought. He came two or three more times. I wondered why he was choosing the times when Rana was home, I couldn't think of a reason other than that he wanted her approval. Yet his last visit turned out to be painful. As soon as Rana opened her mouth, she insulted Talha. Not that she even knew him, even I don't know him. She must have seen them together. Her insult was intended to hurt Mushfik and me. Mushfik laughed, continued talking, but he didn't forget the insult. When he left, I knew he would never come back. Rana had said what she wished to say, made sure Mushfik took note of the new life taking shape inside her womb, and acted as one who'd won the final victory — regardless of how, regardless of what would happen from then on. A few evenings later, when we ran into Mushfik at the theater, he came up and talked to me but did not even look at Rana. I knew why, but neither of them knows that I know. Facing the mirrors, Rana stared first at Mushfik then at Talha. I was watching her from the corner of my eye. But she didn't notice. Then, in the mirror, she and Mushfik caught each other's eye. Mushfik even smiled, almost. Rana made it clear that she saw him and turned her gaze elsewhere. It's all over now. I am still running away. From this mean and ugly story. I am running away from people being used as an excuse for repressed emotions. I don't know where to escape. Does Rana think she accomplished something good? (Yet what's the use of blaming her or myself don't we all knowingly make our mistakes and approach our death step by step doesn't death weigh heavily on our conscience after we have done what we shouldn't have done?)

## RANA

I must admit it now. I must admit what I have been mulling over since last night, what I have been denying all along. I loved Mushfik, rather, I wanted him. Even though I love Sadun and would readily risk my life not to lose him, I realized during that birthday party that I loved Mushfik, I wanted him. He didn't even look at me. No, that's a crass way to put it; instead, he showed me respect, treated me as an older sister; otherwise, I was just another human being, he had no other feeling for me, he harbored none, perhaps because he knew he couldn't, and even if he could, because he wasn't the kind of man who would approach me with bad intentions (as if I wouldn't have accepted the bad intentions! Ah how I wish I weren't here now, how I wish I weren't thinking these thoughts, remembering people, words; I ought to be among the people whom I don't know, whose language I don't understand, dark-skinned people who cross narrow mountain passes, carrying baskets full of fruits on their heads, carrying them to the valley on the other side, oh the astonishing abundance, fruits with unheard-of names and tastes unknown, I ought to be among the people whose language is a birdsong, people who walk half-naked in the heat, who don't miss a single chance to sin despite their blind devotion to God, people who know only the delicious taste of being alive and the fear of God). He loved Sadun, he loved Talha, he loves him still, but he didn't even come near me. I was jealous, but as much for Sadun as for myself. For a year and a half, I couldn't bring myself to confess it openly. Now I can. There is no danger anymore. If Mushfik had continued to visit, maybe something might have happened. But no, even then, nothing would have happened, no, he had to leave.

I saved all of us. I showed them that I was the one holding the strings and playing them however I wanted (because I had to spin a new cocoon a new straitjacket I needed something that would seal me in my solitude as good as water as good as air). I showed them, they discovered my strength, and along with them I discovered my strength as well as my weakness. I was even jealous of Talha although I had no right to be. No, no, it's over now. This has to be my last resolve, that is, if I can withstand my own madness. I must forget Mushfik, not see him again, forget that he exists, I have a child now. My child. He will shelter me against everything, a son, I hope to God. And Sadun will be the man I loved and married. No more Mushfik. Maybe years from now . . . No, I shouldn't leave any doors open. No. That's it. How easy it feels after a year and a half. Mushfik is no more. I am free of him. I saved all of us. I hold the strings. I retreat . . .

(if we meet one day—I still can't help imagining—I will again offer him my hand, forget the mirrors, speak to him, I will again invite him to my house now that I am free, now that we are saved, are we not?)

## LERZAN

Yes, something like jealousy. A lot has happened since this morning, but—the thought stuck in my mind—it was something like jealousy. Whatever else I might have been thinking this morning, I know why I said what I just said. Yes, it was about that one evening, when I was somehow annoyed and couldn't restrain myself. On his way out, Mushfik was promising Talha that they'd meet the next day. I no longer remember my exact words but I did say something to hurt him. But, what good would it do me anyway if I did remember? In those days, I felt that he took over our evenings and mornings, leaving nothing for me. But later the feeling receded, not because I got used to it, I never did. I love Talha like the sunlight, like the soil, the trees, like water. I have no right to be jealous of him because we are bound together. So is everything we hold dear. We can't live without each other. This is our destiny. Why, I don't know, or I know it so well that I no longer need to explain. Like watering the flowers. No need to be afraid. One night, I felt that Mushfik meant not threat, but security. He arrived and sat. Talha wasn't home yet. He would come. We waited. After half an hour, Mushfik seemed restless. At first I thought he was uncomfortable with me. I was almost hurt. But later I realized that he didn't like to be there when Talha wasn't home. Of course, I didn't tell him he was being childish. He was sitting, sunk in the armchair at the other end of the room, getting smaller and smaller, as if he wanted to disappear. Or perhaps he felt shy around me. I wondered if he felt shy around Talha too, but he couldn't have. They were bound by a secret, too. Then it all became clear. The secret between us was entirely different from the one between them. Talha was half of each secret. In this new light, I understood him. Today I can accept this, but it's motherhood that gives me this openness, this forbearance. Regardless of age, motherhood brings women a new wisdom. But as Mushfik has said, I am still afraid of becoming insensitive, jealous, narrow-minded when my son grows older, when he is past seventeen . . . (my son . . .)

That evening, after we waited for quite some time—yes, I recall now, everything happened that evening, until then I was suspicious of Mushfik, one time early in our acquaintance I had asked Talha whether Mushfik was trying some kind of experiment on him, Mushfik seemed so bold and calculating to me, a woman's eye is never fooled, they say, I agreed (that is, it mattered to me whether or not I was fooled, I wanted to be certain) I know Talha, I know how he gets when he loves, I was afraid that Mushfik would want to toy with Talha's feelings—that evening, after we waited for quite some time, after Mushfik shrank and almost disappeared in his seat, he suddenly grew tall, sent the children to bed. I didn't say a word. Now sweetly now sternly, he spoke all the right words and managed to send the children to their bedroom. Then he said, I should leave, Lerzan. Stay a little longer, I said, but he didn't, he got up and left. Less than five minutes after he walked out, the door opened. Talha came in. He was drunk. I had never seen him so drunk in his life. He was falling apart, I'm dying, save me, he kept saying. I thought I was going to faint. Perhaps I could run and catch Mushfik, but I couldn't leave Talha alone. I'm surprised that they didn't see each other on the street. I tried everything I could, finally managed to calm him a little and put him to bed. I am dying, he was saying, hold my hand, I am dissolving, he was saying, yet little by little, his breathing returned to normal. I didn't know where Mushfik lived, otherwise, I would have fetched him. I know that, no matter where or how he was, he would have rushed here. But I didn't know where to find him. I considered a number of places but I couldn't be certain. In the meantime, Talha seemed to feel better, so I stopped thinking about looking for Mushfik. I asked, do you want me to call Mushfik, no, he said, although I'm not sure if he understood my question. How I regretted not knowing where I could find Mushfik. That's when I realized that he meant security. Mushfik did. That day when Talha's anguish drove him to alcohol, one of his old friends was with him. He had left Talha after making him drink so much. Talha had taken a taxi to come home. The following evening, we told all this to Mushfik; he was beside himself with grief. I wish you had called me, he kept saying. Then, when he learned that Talha had come in a taxi, Mushfik began to shake as though he'd been stabbed.

I saw the taxi, he said, I was only a few steps away from the door, I even thought I saw Talha in the backseat, but I thought it odd that Talha would take a taxi to get home, besides, the car didn't stop at the door but a little farther down. Mushfik apparently waited for the person to get out, but when no one did, he continued walking. Talha had been so drunk that he'd had difficulty counting his money, that's why he took a long time getting out. All three of us were pained by this bad luck. In his drunkenness Talha had even missed his own door. (Some other day I might not have believed Mushfik's story; if I were a different person, I might have thought that he had seen Talha and avoided helping him because he didn't want any trouble, but that day I no longer thought so, I knew otherwise.) At times, I was somewhat bothered by Mushfik, but I soon saw my mistake. I also realized that I could trust him. Now everything is fine. Nothing is the matter, I know.

## TALHA

This evening for some reason, Lerzan remembered and mentioned in passing the night when I drank too much and collapsed. I don't know why, is it because she noticed I went out last night? In any case, that's not what really matters. How Mushfik was full of grief the following evening. He had completely forgotten that I had made him wait, that I had drunk until I was as numb as a log, instead, he kept saying, "I should have come back, I should have looked more closely inside the taxi, why didn't you call me?" And why had I drunk so much? Obviously I got carried away. Kemal had kept filling my glass, insisting that I drink, but why did I play along? I was in a vengeful mood, I vaguely remember. As if I wanted to get even with Mushfik. There have been a few other times since then. As if I was doing it to protect myself. But from what, from whom? He never posed a threat to me. That evening, I thought I detected in his grief a strange wish, as though he were thinking: "If he becomes seriously ill, I can have the chance to do something, to help, to offer comfort." This kind of love frightened me. It was nothing other than blind passion. It was fire, the kind that burned, consumed, and still found enough strength to stoke its ashes. Later, I felt ashamed to think like this. He might have thought that momentarily, but if he did, he, too, must have felt shame. Then, another evening, I again felt uneasy. I wanted him and I didn't at the same time. That's when I sensed one of the reasons why. It bothered me that he freely offered all his nights to me. Not because he left me no time to live. I find enough time to live when I'm away from him, and I have told him as much. Besides, our life together is a separate life, different, it is neither his nor mine, but ours. Each moment, a separate, inextinguishable life. Even when he comes to our house and forces this other life on me in front of Lerzan and the children, even when he takes me away from them—and in the midst of them—he always remains respectful of my home; this shouldn't bother me either, especially since I live the other life willingly, feel it, distill it drop by drop in my being. (Yet it bothered me that he offered his nights to me, no, it frightened me, I mustn't be afraid of admitting that it frightened me . . . It was the fear of "if one day," as he often called it. And how many times has he told me that it was a pleasant fear, I know it, I know it, too.) He always says that if a person is capable of loving this intensely, then he must cast the fear out, he must live, he must only live, he must cast out all the seeds of death bound to overwhelm life. I am aware of the fear, yet sometimes I realize that I cannot cast it out altogether. Always the same fear of "if one day." It's futile, I know, I have accepted it, yet . . . (yet there is the desert, the thousand-year-old time, there is solitude, the elusive futility of all effort to fool solitude, there is the desire to return, to escape, to remain alone, there is the yellow sand, the fathomless blue and no color mixed in between . . . there is, yet . . .) the fear remains. As he says, casting out the fear shouldn't mean shutting your eyes and creating a false sense of security. This life, these sentiments must be sifted through, scrutinized daily; far from falling asleep, one must throb with sleeplessness, but away from the fear, no, not away, beyond (away from the thousand-year-old fear the mossy slippery darkness away not even away beyond where the darkness itself is lost from memory) in a place where the fear is unknown.

We drank again, it's been a few days (no only three days but so much has happened since then that it feels longer) we drank and put aside our misgivings. I spoke first, I'm not sure why, but I wanted to tell him that the house suffocated me at times. Perhaps I didn't explain it well, but we understood each other. I didn't mean suffocated, I wanted to describe the occasional feeling of being fettered. I always have trouble describing such matters (he grows impatient with me when I tell him that, if you can't describe them, he says, if you say you can't describe them, then who can, shall we ask those who don't know the burden of words, he says, I tell him, maybe it's because I know and feel the burden that I can't describe them, maybe because I want to escape, because I am aware, so is he, you're crazy, he says, laughing). But that night we couldn't laugh, we were living our life, we were inside it, we had thrown overboard the subtlety and the conceit of laughter. The sea mattered more. At first our conversation was normal, we searched to understand each other, but gradually we made it to the heart of the matter. I listened. He was talking about me. I listened. Then I said, you were searching for some things, you were ready to find them, I said, then I appeared before you, you were ready so you found in me what you were looking for, I said, what you found, what you wanted to see in me, you were ready to see. I didn't know how he would respond. I had handed him one end of the rope, I was holding the other end, he would either pull it to undo the knot or tighten it even more. He nodded. I waited. Yes, he said, perhaps I was ready—the rope stretched—perhaps I was ready to find—the rope began slipping—but not in you—the rope tightened. Perhaps we should call it a coincidence, he said. Yes, a coincidence, but everything shaping our lives is a coincidence. You are a coincidence, and so am I. Let's not play with words. Why not call it God instead. In any case, he said, it was a coincidence in one way or another, but would I have found what I was looking for without you, perhaps I was ready, but . . . There was a but—the rope hung between our hands. He tightened the knot the next evening (he always does this, why should I mind?) while walking in the street. We were silent. Suddenly he uttered my name into the darkness, Talha, he said, last night I was an ass when I said maybe I was ready, when I said it was a coincidence; I was right when I called it God; I thought about it all night, I was searching, yes, but I wasn't ready to find it, just as I wasn't ready to find you. I was simply searching, I probably didn't even know what I was searching for, I only had a sense of it. But I found it in you. I recognized it when I found it but it felt odd, not in a bad way, more like the odd feeling one experiences when an overcast sky suddenly breaks open, and one sees a single beautiful cloud suspended in the pure blue, the way the blue feels odd. Had I been ready, it wouldn't have felt odd. But the joy that followed clarified everything (a light drizzle a warm quiet calm drizzle he lifted his head and repeated again—I don't know how many times he had already repeated—you made me love the rain now at least when I am with you I love being rained on my hair my eyes my lips we both loved the rain). But the night before, when he had left the rope hanging loose and said none of this, he had instead brought up the subject of jealousy. On account of our separate life and those left outside it. He had mentioned those who can't endure love, those who are terrified, and quite unexpectedly, he had brought up Judas, tried to explain him. His account was jumbled but slowly a light began to shine through his words. I wanted to be washed in that light. Love had to be the way he described it (the way I knew it too but couldn't articulate love beyond all silence). He was released from death, he had found the feeling of oneness against all the dualities. His eyes filled with tears, glistening, his tears traced a path to his chin. I didn't turn my face away for a long time, we were held in each other's gaze . . .

He should be here any minute. I should free myself. (release erupt I should expel the molten remains of years I will soon begin I will awaken the fire that has laid dormant for months it will awaken itself it will empty out flow unsilent I will leave and transfigure myself into words sounding from the heart of time . . .)

## DILAVER

He is late again tonight, he won't come for dinner. Yet when he left this morning, he behaved as though he had forgotten about last night. He hugged me. Dear mother, he kept calling me. Asked me for all sorts of things. I know his spoiled childish side. Is he doing all this because he knows it pleases me or does he enjoy it when I serve him, sometimes I can't tell. But, no, I should be able to tell; often, he cannot think of any other way to show he loves me (at times I am amazed how well he knows love, is this how he loved everyone he's loved in his life?). It's the same with me, but I know that this is what I want. Still, after being so sweet this morning, why didn't he come home for dinner? Did something happen, did he remember something again, or is he angry? (That's how my life was spent I always thought of him what's left for me after all is said and done.) I wonder if he went to Talha. If so, he wouldn't even think of me, or even if he did, he wouldn't leave him and come home. I gave up waiting for him and ate. I forced the morsels down my throat. Otherwise, he gets upset, Do you want to become sick by starving yourself? he asks.

How can I want to eat when he is not here? If he was really worried that I don't eat without him, then he wouldn't skip a meal. If he truly thought of me. Maybe he is sincere, maybe he does think of me but just can't bring himself to leave Talha's side. Talha . . . I must admit, I have seen enough of Mushfik's other friends, none compares with Talha, yes, I am certain, even I trust him, but why steal every one of our evenings like this? True, it's not clear whether Talha is doing the stealing, Mushfik is my son, I should know his ways. (Talha has been exceptional for Mushfik, even I can tell, he was never attached like this before, it's entirely different, like the long-forgotten friendships of old). I ought to try and finish this food. He won't come. Who knows at what godforsaken hour I'll hear the door open, recognize the sound of keys dropping into his pocket, wait for him to come to my room and turn off my lamp, feel his hands lift off my glasses, take the book from my pillow, listen to him lie down in his bed, to the sound of his sleep? In the morning when he is still asleep, I'll stand by his bed, watch him sleep. My son. Whatever he does, whatever happens . . . my son . . . Yet how I wish, dear God, he were willing to give me a bit more of Talha's time . . .

**MUSHFIK**

What is he doing now? I hope he doesn't rush out to the street because I'm late. I'm running. If I can catch up with him, I have things to say, I must say them, I must see him.

I hear his voice behind the door. Now I can catch my breath.

What I had to say seemed the usual minutiae, but they were significant minutiae. I was careful not to mention last night. The topic did come up once but we quickly moved away from it. I only told him I'd been distressed and wandered in the dark, under the trees, he said he had also gone out. Did you come by my house, I asked, afraid, no, he said, I didn't want to see anybody. I was pleased.

Had he come by and not found me at home, I would have been sad. Yet I would also have derived some satisfaction from knowing that he had come in the middle of the night, looking for me. This time determined to wake me . . .

No, my mind was elsewhere. All of a sudden I told him, sometimes you don't want to see me. How so? he asked. Just so, I said, I can't explain it now, although I also take back what I just said, I take it back because when you mentioned my mother—seized with foolish fears like me—you told me not to leave her alone too much. Perhaps that's why he didn't want to see me, I didn't tell him this, although I wondered. Yes, it seems to me that he distances himself, at times finds all kinds of excuses to avoid seeing me (I know I shouldn't forget that even when thinking about it himself he doesn't acknowledge it rather it's his sense of guilt that pierces him sometimes I see it in his face in his hands in his eyes I shouldn't forget since I can't avoid drowning in my own selfishness either) sometimes I sense he is afraid of holding me, I understand, I want to explain that it's childish. But then I change my mind. Because I feel that way too from time to time, the same fear of holding him, of chaining him. (I would have liked to tell him that his feeling his sense of guilt its piercing surge all are futile that he is causing nothing but unnecessary grief for himself but am I any different?)

When he told me that he wished I wouldn't leave my mother alone too much, I looked into his eyes, I agree, I said, but it shouldn't mean we have to give up living our own life. I noticed a glow in his eyes, an icy glow. Neither of us looked away. We were held together like this, too.

He is happier when he meets me alone, he wants us to meet alone, I know. Yet if this becomes a habit, it will turn into another form of escape. We mustn't escape, we must hone ourselves for life. One evening we talked about those who escape—it was the same evening when he told me "you were ready to find"—we said, there are those who escape and those who search for a shelter and find it by wandering under the vast sky. But those who escape, perhaps they know where they escape from but never where they want to escape to. Why should we resemble them? We should do nothing that resembles escape. Even this joy of being alone mustn't be worth escaping for. Sometimes I want to escape, too. I was the one who told him—Talha—not to make her—my mother—talk about the old days, and when he did, I was the one who gently but resolutely urged him to change the subject. Mother reminisces about the old days only in tears; I keep her from talking so she doesn't feel sad, yes, she still feels sad when she is not allowed to talk but not as much. I asked the same thing from Talha too. But in asking, didn't I also want Talha to remain a stranger to those stories, to that past? Sometimes I want to escape, too (from everything I know from everything I don't know). I must escape, too. After I find shelter . . .

## TALHA

Why did he bring up selfishness tonight? Who would know better than he that we are far from being selfish? Beneath all sorts of acts that resemble selfishness, there is something entirely different (beneath all those acts of his that resemble selfishness). What seems like selfishness is instead the result of putting one's self in the center and realigning the rest of the world according to this self. It is about perceiving everything, including one's self, from within one's heart. I, too, could have done the same. But I don't. Instead I, too, seem to perceive him as the world's center. (soon words will come soon very soon I too will be transfigured into words into the past soon the most vital riddles yet unsolved between us will make themselves known because we are strong now we can begin now soon the age of riddles will begin the age of solving riddles will begin everything that is above and beyond all our conversations everything that we both touched upon but avoided everything that is vital neither to me nor to him but to us) And I perceive his words as my starting point. But why did selfishness cross his mind all of a sudden? It was an old subject. But it crosses his mind, it does, isn't this, in a way, what he means by sifting, scrutinizing life? (except that he is not waiting for the time that is soon to begin he is not waiting even though it was he who wanted and awaited the words that would illuminate the darkness I know he'll be surprised but we are strong now we ought to be strong I may falter so may he but faltering too will end even though it now seems as endless as the seasons we ought to be strong)

## MUSHFIK

I wanted to say that I have, that we have, transcended selfishness, I know it's unnecessary, but I had to. Perhaps he doesn't know yet what I am trying to say. Not yet, but soon I will be able to say it openly, unflinchingly, without fear. How I have, how we have transcended selfishness, ugliness. He doesn't know, perhaps it will be difficult to begin, but I must tell him how he is beyond all measure, we are stronger now, we have to be, I will tell him soon. I mentioned self-ishness often tonight, circled around it. Soon everything will begin.

Yet, he knows I would stay put for the rest of my life rather than go anywhere he is not. The other day, when we were again talking about leaving, about traveling and I said, you know the reason why I won't leave, didn't he say, I'll come along, we'll leave together just so you can leave? He can't go, neither can I, but didn't those words come out of his mouth?

We are strong now, hoping.

1956

**Bilge Karasu** (1930-1995) was one of Turkey's most inventive and beloved writers. His work has been translated and published widely throughout Europe. His novel *Night* (Louisiana University Press) was published in English translation in 1994 and won the Pegasus Prize for Literature. This is his second work to be translated into English.

**Aron Aji** is Professor of Literature at Butler University-Indianapolis. A native of Izmir, Turkey, he has translated several works by the Turkish authors Murathan Mungan, Latife Tekin and Güney Dal. He is currently at work on a translation of Bilge Karasu's *The Garden of Migrant Cats,* which will be published by New Directions Press.